STEPBROTHER

ANONYMOUS

ARIA COLE

STEPBROTHER ANONYMOUS

Copyright © 2017 by Aria Cole

Model: Tyler Halligan
Photographer: Wander Aguiar

Cover Design: Sybil at PopKitty Design
Editing: Silently Correcting Your Grammar

Love is for suckers.

That's always been Hudson Farrow's take on it. His mother has practically made a career out of saying *I do*, which is why he's found himself in another upstate town, preparing to watch her walk down the aisle with another yacht club asshole, nursing his cynicism with scotch at another lonely dive bar. A sassy siren that sets his blood on fire wasn't part of the plan, neither was a new stepsister, and now Hudson's a man with a problem because he's just found out they're one in the same.

Skylar Walsh never thought the one and only man she's ever brought home would turn into anything beyond a few orgasms. Until six-foot-four, sinfully sexy, talented and tattooed sweeps her off her feet—*and right between his thighs*—on his custom Harley. When Hudson demands her phone number before the night even begins she knows she's in for a wild ride. When she runs into him at her father's wedding the next day, she realizes she may have just made the biggest mistake of her life. A dozen sheet-clenching, toe-curling, and soul-shatteringly good mistakes in the last twenty-four hours.

Warning: Hudson is hell-bent on his Sky, and he won't let a little thing like *I do* come between them. Filthy-sweet tattooed hearts, perfectly placed piercings that hit all the right spots, and love and fate inked so deep no force can keep them apart--hold onto your hearts because *Stepbrother Anonymous* stole mine! *xo Aria*

One

Hudson

"Two fingers of top-shelf Scotch," I murmured at the bartender, anxious for the dark liquid to quiet my head. He poured a few ounces, sliding the glass across the bar with a nod. I tipped the glass of amber amnesia to my lips, the booze easing a little more of the tension out of my shoulders. My neck. Fuck, I'd been wound tight in the weeks before I even had to make this trip.

I finished the glass, setting it back on the bar and nodding to the bartender. Another upstate asshole—why did my mother always find herself around these types of people?

I swear, sometimes she tried to find herself by marrying someone new. This was her fourth wedding, not that I was judging, but she'd picked some real losers before.

I'd had my fair share of shitty stepdads, so when she'd called a few months ago and told me she was getting married—again—I'd shoved it to the back of my mind.

If I could have avoided this wedding, I sure as hell would have.

But she was my mother, despite all the dysfunction,

and I wasn't the kind of man to leave my own mother flapping in the wind.

Thankfully, she and the new beau weren't going traditional with a wedding party—I'd been forced to step into a monkey suit at the age of fifteen when she'd married the last one, and I'd fucking hated every minute.

She was lucky I was here; that was about all the enthusiasm I could muster.

The bartender replenished my whiskey, nodding at me before tapping on the wooden bar to my left, a grin crossing his face that could only be reserved for a woman. A good-looking one.

I knew men, and I knew there must be one helluva piece standing next to me.

I took a sip of my drink, glancing out of the corner of my eye to find a woman next to me, waves of auburn hair falling around her shoulders and eyes so big and wide I nearly swallowed my own tongue.

"I'll have whatever he's having." She gestured to the glass in my hand.

A smile spread over my cheeks. "You sure about that? This'll create a fire in your belly."

"Bring it, then." Her eyes darted up to mine, leveling on me and ripping all the sense from my mind. Ice-blue oceans swirled back at me. I was sure I'd never seen eyes quite that color.

"Woman who handles her liquor, I'm intrigued." I took another sip, enjoying the way her eyes hovered on my lips with each of my words.

"You'd be surprised what I can handle." The bartender deposited her drink on the bar top. "Cheers to a good weekend."

I clinked my glass with hers then watched as she took

a healthy swallow. My eyebrows rose and my grin deepened.

This woman had fire, and hell if I wasn't drawn to her flame.

"I'm going to need another one." She set the glass on the bar when she'd finished.

"Well, hell, remind me not to go underestimating you again."

"Again?" She cocked her head to the side, a pretty, sarcastic as hell grin darting across her lips. When she did that, I couldn't help wanting to cover her mouth with mine, lick up the dips and swells of her body, and make her scream and shudder around me. My dick twitched in my pants, demanding to be let loose and cradled in her warmth. "What makes you think you'll get a chance at again?"

Sweet fucking Jesus, she had sass. Sassy women were the sexiest to me. There was something about this woman; something that made me want to bend her over and spank that fine ass until she begged me to stop by shoving my rock-hard cock deep into her wet, warm cunt. Just the very idea of that made me feverish.

I'd begun to think I should find myself a nice quiet little thing. Maybe opposites really did attract, and I was barking up the wrong tree when a girl like this one flashed her big, beautiful eyes at me. But damned if I could help it. I was having a visceral reaction just standing so close to her.

"Won't be the last if I have anything to say about it."

"You don't." She smiled up at me sweetly, winking once before taking another swallow of her newly refreshed drink. Hell, was I looking at the female version of myself? I didn't know if I should be turned on or run the hell away, but she was intriguing, and no way was I walking away from someone intriguing this weekend. I'd need all the distraction I could get before heading back to the city and my life and putting this marriage business behind me.

I wished the best for my mom, but she'd sort of ruined the idea of commitment for me.

Never could bring myself to say those three words, though I didn't sweat it. My life was good. What was the point of giving your heart away to someone who inevitably would only break it? My mother was proof enough. I'd seen her in broken relationships time and time again. I didn't want any part of it. People weren't built to last, and true love was a mirage the media distorted in order to sell you more junk you didn't need.

But I had a feeling things would get a little bit better if I got to know this woman.

"Name's Hudson."

Her grin deepened, sky-blue eyes sparkling up at me. "Skylar Walsh."

"Can I get you another drink, Skylar?"

She paused, eyes narrowing adorably before she replied, "Why? Because I'm the nearest thing with boobs?"

Her candid words took me by surprise and forced a chuckle from me. "Because you're the only woman who's made me care enough to ask her name in a long time, Skylar." I pushed a stray lock of hair behind her ear. "Figure that counts for something."

Her pupils darkened, lips pressed together before she turned back to the bartender and nodded at him for another. "Smooth talker, then, huh?"

"Call it what you want, but I say what's on my mind."

"I can see that." She took a small sip of her drink then set it back on the bar, turning fully to me.

I'd been so focused on her eyes that I hadn't even bothered to check out the rest of her, and the rest of her was fucking sinful.

She was the curviest, most beautiful creature I'd ever seen, and living in a city overrun with trendy singles, I'd seen a lot.

None that had caught me off guard quite like this, though.

"What's on your mind, Hudson?"

I inched closer, brushing her shoulder with mine and sucking in a deep breath of her heady aroma. "I'm thinkin' the drive up this weekend was damn well worth it, after all."

Her lips popped open in surprise, warmth creeping up her neck and making me desperate to touch her searing hot skin. Was she as aroused as I was? Did she feel this push and pull careening between us?

"Well, what can we do to make your trip worthwhile, Hudson?" The soft lilt of her tone told me she knew exactly what effect she had on me.

"I can think of a few things," I breathed, taking advantage of the low light and sliding in a little closer. I was drawn to her like a magnet, our bodies hovering just at the edge of contact, close enough to drive us both a little insane. Skylar closed her eyes, a soft shiver racing through her body when my fingers darted across the sweet flesh of her thigh. "I bet you taste sweet."

Her eyes fluttered closed, long lashes shadowing her high cheekbones. For the first time in my life, I couldn't think of anything but the gorgeous woman standing in front of me, her body attuned to mine. I had to know her. Something told me I was flirting with forever with this one. I couldn't put my finger on why, but I sure as hell felt it. Like our souls were already chained together, just waiting for the bodies to catch up.

I wanted tonight with her, but I wanted all the other nights too. I wanted to figure out what made her laugh, what made her mad, what turned her on. I really wanted that last part.

"I'm not sure if your unfiltered mouth pisses me off or turns me on." She arched one eyebrow, leaning in a little closer.

"My bet's on the latter with the way your thighs shift and your nipples are aching under that dress."

Her lips curved up then as she leaned a little closer, the generous swell of her gorgeous tits brushing the rock-hard slab of my chest. "Wouldn't you like to know."

Sweet mother of God, I was a goner with this one.

Two

Skylar

Three hours after I walked into the bar, I was walking out of it, my arm linked with the sexiest, most infuriating human I'd ever met. The drop-dead gorgeous and cocky sonuvabitch had latched on, and I was surprised that I didn't want him to let go.

Dating wasn't my thing. Growly, irritating macho men weren't my thing either, but this guy was both and all at once, so why the hell did my stomach turn flips every time a word came out of his mouth?

"Hop on." Hudson held his hand out, the other on the handle of a glossy black Harley-Davidson. As if the dark tattoos licking his forearms and the gauge in one ear weren't enough, this guy riding a motorcycle cemented every ounce of his bad boy persona.

"You've got a bike?"

"Rode it hard all the way up here." His eyes sparked as he watched me. Something spiraled up in my belly, arousal and need coursing through my veins and leaving me at the mercy of his every whim.

"I've never been on a motorcycle before." I grasped his hand with mine.

"Not just any motorcycle, princess. A Harley—best of the best. You can feel the power between your thighs."

"Sounds sexy."

"Unbelievably sexy," he agreed, eyes crisscrossing my body before landing on my gaze again. "Climb on."

Excitement unfurled inside me, his touch like lightning bolts shooting along my nerves and gathering at the juncture of my thighs. "Am I safe with you?"

His grin slid sideways, eyes holding mine for unwavering beats, silence pulsing between us. "You'll never be safer than you are with me, Sky, that I can promise you." One hand cupped my neck, drawing me to him. "I'd lose a limb before I'd let anything happen to you."

His words bloomed slowly in my heart, filling up all the dark corners and making me believe in him. Truly believe. A guy who looked like that wasn't one you should believe, but here I was—a lamb blindly going to my slaughter.

I'd always considered myself good at reading people, and while this guy was a little hard to decipher in some respects, the possessive aura radiated off of him. There wasn't a bone in his body that could hurt another human being; I could feel it as much as I could see it.

"YOLO, I guess." I slung one leg over the machine with his help, surprised when he followed me on, his hard body coming to press against my back.

"I thought you were driving?" I teased.

"I am." His rough hands latched on to my waist and spun me in the seat, tucking my knees between his powerful thighs and the leather of the seat. His hands cupped my face, eyes focused on the soft part of my lips as I wondered what to say, what he wanted from me, what tomorrow would look like. I'd told myself earlier it was okay if this was just a one-night stand. I'd never had one, and the chaos that had been my life of late could really use a release.

But in reality, the idea of this guy walking away tomorrow morning filleted me open a little bit. I would never be a clinger—I had a career, a life, a home I loved —but something about him told me this was more. Told me that if he walked away, it would leave me shattered.

Would the pleasure be worth it? If the way he was looking at me was any indication, like he wanted to eat me alive, then I had a feeling it one thousand percent would be.

"I need to taste you first." His lips crashed to mine, not gentle—frantic. Like he'd been starved for this moment.

God, I think I had been too.

My hands wound around his neck, my lips opening as his tongue pushed past and tangled with mine. With every heartbeat, passion flowed from me to him, his hands eating up my skin, his breath fanning across my face. He'd been right earlier when he'd said I was turned on. I was practically a hot mess in his presence. Sitting on the front of his bike with his lips attached to mine now was the most recklessly hedonistic thing I'd ever done, and I was quickly becoming addicted.

His lips never left mine when he caged me in his arms, then kick-started the bike to leave. It roared underneath me, causing all the aroused blood in my body to charge straight for my already wet pussy. I was a mess, but I couldn't be bothered to care when his body was still pressed against mine, his tongue fucking me slow and deep as the motorcycle engine purred beneath us.

He tore his lips away for one moment before slowly guiding the bike out of the parking spot, turning it, and then shooting out of the parking lot, hovering at the end of the driveway leading into our quiet town.

"Which way, precious?" My brain fried as it registered what I was doing. Letting this man take me home tonight. A stranger, a roguish, sexy, motorcycle-riding man who'd charmed the panties right off of me. But I still didn't care.

"Right. Go left at the first stop sign, and my house is a few doors down on the left," I said in a quick breath, before my logical, safety-minded self kicked in and politely declined the offer. Told him I was a good girl who didn't do these things and went home alone.

And I was a good girl, too much of the time. So much of the time, it got exhausting, and a spike of adrenaline raced through my bloodstream, begging me to do something reckless, something just mine. Something in the name of pure pleasure.

"I can't wait to get you underneath me." He drove one-handed, his other palm coming to rest on my thigh, thumb inching higher and higher, kneading at the flesh until I thought I might come in a scream right that very second.

"I can hardly think straight with your hands on my skin."

"That's what I had in mind." He nipped at my ear, leaning as he turned the bike left, and I registered we were almost home. To my place. To my bed.

Anticipation built inside me, my legs already quivering as the pad of his thumb inched nearer to my panties. I sucked in a breath of the cool night air, disbelieving any of this was happening right now.

And then his thumb breached my panties.

The rough scrape of his fingertip against my hot flesh was like a shot of cold water dousing my body. I clamped my teeth on my lip, thighs shaking as his thumb stroked back and forth, my pussy growing wetter with every pass. He added a second finger, working it at my entrance before sliding in smoothly, my body welcoming him with more silky hot arousal.

"I'm so fucking hard, feeling your beautiful little pussy wrapped around my finger. You are so wet, so responsive. I know you love the feel of my fingers in your pussy. You're soaked. I want to taste that pussy, Sky, I want to get drunk on that sweet juice." His words edged at my ear. "You want me inside you. Owning this sweet cunt."

Like fireworks exploding in my chest cavity, waves of release pulsed their way through every muscle I possessed. My fingers clutched at his firm biceps, shades of ink swirling across the hard muscle, as my teeth clenched down and I rode the orgasm with the help of his frantically moving hand between my legs.

"Oh my God, I've never—" I sucked in shallow breaths of air. "I can't believe—"

His grin crooked to one side as he pulled his hand from between my legs, sucking his thumb into his mouth and licking the nectar clean. "Your pussy tastes sweet, Skylar."

His words embarrassed me and turned me on in equal measure. He must have known, because his grin ticked up just as his bike began to slow down. "Which house is yours?"

Drowsy and drunk on pleasure, I hardly recognized my neighborhood, veiled in shadows.

"Uh, 331." I spat the number, unable to even think

about providing direction at this moment.

A slow chuckle rumbled through his chest, sending shock waves through me. I'd never been so turned on, so sated and needy for him all at the same time.

"Welcome home, precious." His throaty voice curled around my body as he turned into my driveway. The engine flicked off, and he smiled.

Three

Hudson

Before we could even make it to her bedroom, I flipped her in my arms and bent her over the kitchen island. Her gaze nailed mine just as my hands were sliding up the creamy skin of her thighs, damp and still shaking from the first orgasm I'd nursed from her.

"You're so turned on for me you can't even keep still, precious," I crooned at her ear, using the moment of distraction to tear her panties down her legs. She sighed, ass working back and forth like it was begging for my teeth. My bite mark on her pretty ass would look nice, a brand on her skin. I was determined to give her that and more.

I pushed the hem of her dress over the round globes of her sweet ass and sank my teeth into one cheek, enjoying the shudder that coursed through her, dampening her thighs and turning my cock to steel. Beads of precome dotted the front of my jeans as I lowered to my knees and plunged my tongue into her pretty pink flesh.

Lapping and sucking at her soaked lips, I swirled and tasted and savored every drop of herself she had to give.

I wanted her so fucking wet for me she wouldn't be able to think straight when I slid into her the first time.

Fisting at the cheeks of her ass, I shoved my face deeper, coating it with her juices, smearing her on my lips, covering myself in her scent because here, with her, was the only place I ever wanted to be.

She arched when I slid one slow finger into her body, nearly losing myself when her walls contracted around me, sucking me in and begging for more. She groaned when I nipped at the hard little bud of her clit. Sliding one hand up the curve of her hips, I locked her hand in mine, holding her tightly as I sucked that little nub into my mouth and danced figure eights around it with my tongue. Her legs tensed, her breathing growing more erratic, before I hooked my fingers and sent her straight over the edge and into my arms.

Her muscles seized up around me, arousal coursing down my chin and drenching my fingers. I'd done my job well, all right. I'd made her come so hard she'd never be able to fuck anyone else without thinking of where I'd been.

Just as her breathing calmed, I spun her in my arms, still on my knees, and lifted her skirt, lapping at the moisture coating her thighs. She shuddered when I slid my tongue up the seam of her pretty cunt, sucking all the stray honey from her skin and savoring the essence of her on my taste buds. I could go for being surrounded by her scent every night and live a long and happy life.

One of her hands pushed into my hair as I worked her into a frenzy, the skirt of her dress falling in silky waves around me. "I need to see you naked and spread out before me. I need to see what I am eating for dinner and dessert."

I stood, grasping the dress and pulling it over her shoulders. She stood, all soft and creamy in the silvery moonlight, panty-free and only a pretty purple bra edged in lace preventing my mouth from reaching the Promised Land.

"You're so fucking beautiful, precious, I don't know what to eat next." But I knew where I was headed, my hands already pulling the bra from her body and stripping her bare. Her nipples puckered in the brisk night, but I didn't give them long without my attention. My hands were embracing her tits, my mouth covering one nipple and drawing in long sucks. Her hands threaded through my hair as soft little moans fell from her lips.

Christ, those moans would be the death of me.

She had to stop making those noises, or I'd never last as long as I needed to last to please her in all the ways I wanted to.

"Where's the bed?" I grunted, hauling her into my arms and wrapping her thighs around my hips. She rode my denim-covered cock like that a few steps before I realized it was no fucking good at all. "Too far."

I set her down onto the couch underneath me, her body laid out, tits full, thighs creamy and begging for my hands clutching as I plowed into her.

Her hands were at my button, working the metal back and forth before I grew frustrated with all the fabric between us and pulled the zipper down in one quick stroke. Shoving the denim down my thighs, I grunted with equal parts pain and relief when my cock hit the cool air.

I needed inside her before I lost my head.

Hell, I think I had already lost it.

"Oh my God," she gasped into the moonlit night. "You're pierced."

A sideways grin turned my lips. "Want a better look?"

Her eyebrow shot up, a small smile turning her full lips. Fuck, I wanted those lips around my cock, the tip hitting the back of her throat as my rough hands pushed through her hair. I wanted everything with this woman.

"It looks amazing." She dragged one finger up the thick vein that throbbed from the base to the tip, one painted nail dusting across the metal bar that pierced the ridge of my cock.

"Wait until you feel it." I cupped her fist around my shaft, the tip already leaking thick beads of precome at just the thought of being buried inside of her.

"I'm not on anything," she confessed. "But I might have a condom in my bathroom."

I growled, the idea of a single scrap of anything coming between us more than I was willing to handle. "Not tonight, precious. Tonight's just you and me. I'm so fucking squeaky clean I can show you my test results on my phone right now."

"I believe you." Her hands cupped my cheeks, drawing me in for a slow kiss. "I believe you, Hudson."

Her legs locked around my waist then, the tip of my cock sliding against her entrance and sending stars rocketing behind my vision, that little ball of metal doing its job and rubbing her and me in all the right places.

"Jesus, woman." I laid my forehead against hers, sucking in one long breath as my mind raged. I hovered at her entrance, everything in me wanting to plow in, claim what was mine, but I had to show her this was more. How could I show her this didn't just end here?

"Give me your phone number," I demanded, fishing

my own phone out of my jeans pocket.

"What?" she moaned, lips working against my ear and sending me on a delicious path to pleasure and destruction.

"I'm not fucking you until you know what this means to me."

"What does it mean?" she murmured, fingertips dancing across my shoulders.

"It means you can't run out on me. It means we wake up in the morning, and you're mine just as much as you are right now." I closed her lips with a forceful kiss, showing her exactly what I meant. "I like you all quivering and needy underneath me, precious. I like knowing I own your orgasms and that pretty pink pussy."

Her sparkling baby blues flared. I help up my phone, waiting patiently, my dick teasing just close enough to touch but not nearly enough to provide any release. I had to get what I wanted first, and what I wanted was her—tomorrow...and all the rest of the days.

"Give me what I want, and you get what you want." I dragged my dick along the hot seam of her cunt, enjoying the shudder that burned through her.

"That little barbell..." she whispered.

"Is amazing. Wait until you feel it scraping against your clit." I plucked at her nipple.

In one quick breath, she rattled off her phone number, and luckily, I was fast enough to catch it all before hitting save and dumping my phone on the floor. "I find out that's a bogus number, I will find a way to punish you."

"Punished?" Her eyes locked on mine, lip caught between her teeth. "What kind of punishment?"

"Whatever I can think of to make you wither in pain and in pleasure." I snaked a hand around her neck, holding her firmly as I touched our lips, kissing her slowly, tentatively, my dick sliding a little harder, a little deeper with each pass.

Her nails dug into my sides, her breath washing across my neck in desperate pants, and then finally I slipped in. And lost in her body, swimming with her soul, I fucking came alive.

With frantic thrusts, I clutched at her hips, rocking her against me as we worked a steady rhythm together. Her fingers grasped at my flesh, leaving fiery nail tracks in their wake. My teeth clung to her neck, sucking at the hollow and laving up the line of her throat before she was gasping and begging for more.

More of me.

More of us.

Sweet fucking Jesus, I think I was on the verge of losing my mind.

"Oh my God, that piercing," she moaned. "Thank you Jesus for that piercing."

Her words drove me on, sure I'd hit that button buried deep inside when her tight cunt quivered around my already sensitive cock.

"You like that, baby? You like the way I fuck you with that piercing?" I dragged in and out, the sighs from her lips urging me on. "I love feeling how wet you are for me. My pussy wants to come, doesn't it? You want to gush all over my thick cock, don't you? I can't wait to see your sexy face while you taste yourself on my cock. I'm going to have you every which way, precious. I'm going to own every sexy inch of you," I husked, angling her hips so I could hit a deeper spot. "I'm going to tie you up and make you mine." I placed a kiss on her mouth. "You make me want things I didn't know I ever wanted before."

I tugged at the long waves of her hair, pulling her head back to mine in a possessive kiss. She moaned against my lips, causing an orgasm to barrel through my spine. Holding myself taut over her, I emptied into her sexy little body, wishing for a split second that my seed would coat her unprotected womb and plant my baby right where it belonged.

Skylar and I tied together for life sounded pretty goddamn perfect right now.

My release ebbed, my cock not even starting to soften before my hands were massaging her scalp, slipping her over to straddle me bare on the couch. Planting kisses on her neck, chest, across those pert little nipples, I doused myself in her. I could overdose on her body and die a happy man.

"You're like a drug, Skylar." I hummed the words at her ear.

Her body arched, nipples puckering, before I planted my mouth on hers again.

I couldn't get lost in the words. I only had feelings to give to her, and we weren't anywhere near done yet.

Fucking Skylar felt like touching a live wire. I'd never held much respect for words like love and forever, but if this was as close as I ever got to it, I'd know that for just one night I'd touched fire, and I'd lived to tell the tale.

Four

Skylar

I woke the following morning, my thighs sore, my lips bruised, and a headache the size of Texas pounding through my head. Flopping a pillow over my throbbing head to block the morning light, I did not expect a rough palm to slither its way across my bare abdomen, down my thighs, until it cupped my warm cunt.

Oh God.

Every forbidden piece of last night came rushing back to me. Tall, tattooed, arrogant, motorcycle-riding, and tucked into my bed at this very moment.

"Morning, precious." His words wound around my insides like rivers of molten lava.

"Hi," I breathed, suddenly a little self-conscious.

"Cat got your tongue?" I finally chanced a glance at him. That cocky grin was twisting his lips. Fuck, no wonder I'd fallen so far down the rabbit hole last night. He looked even better in the morning, and I didn't even think that was possible.

"No cat." I cleared my throat, slipping out of bed and walking into the bathroom. I was hoping he wouldn't follow so I could have a few minutes to freak out in the bathroom mirror before I faced this day, but luck was apparently not on my side today.

He sauntered into my bathroom, just like he belonged there, my gaze landing for the first time on a vertical trail of inked words decorating his rib cage. I couldn't make out what they said, the only thought running through my head that I wanted to drop to my knees and lick my way up the art climbing every taut muscle of his body.

Never in my life had I found myself in a morning-after situation until now, until six-foot-tall and fucking gorgeous snaked his heavily inked arms around my waist and placed a warm kiss at my neck. "Shower with me?"

Oh God, what was I supposed to say to that? No, actually, I'd rather sit here and lick my wounds alone, thank you very much.

"You weren't so shy last night." His spicy, leathery scent wrapped around me, nearly buckling my knees.

"Scotch does that to me," I muttered, eyes lingering on the sea of skulls that wrapped around his elbow, twisted up his bicep, and sprayed across one shoulder. His body was a work of art, and holding a conversation when he was just standing there…*like this*…all naked and gorgeous and mouthwatering was fucking impossible.

"So…" He twirled me in his broad arms to face him. "You've done this before?"

My eyes widened as I realized what he was asking. "No." I shook my head with a huff. "Never. But I'm usually out drinking with my girlfriends, and we have this pact that we're not allowed to go home with anyone for safety…" I paused, eyes landing on his again. "…reasons."

"Right." He cupped my face in his hands, forcing me to look only at him. "Well, I've got news for you, doll.

I've never done this sort of shit either, and while the bright light of day may have changed your view, it hasn't mine."

He paused, letting his words loom heavy between us.

"And that means what?" I finally asked, afraid of his answer.

"It means I had a taste, and now I'm addicted. Not walking away from you, precious, and you're sure as hell not walking away from me." His heavy hands splayed across my shoulders, hauling me to him and crushing me into a possessive kiss. On instinct, my hands whispered into his hair, my body molding to his like it was meant to be there, our tongues twisting and stroking in tantalizing loops.

I should be pushing him away. Everything about his attitude made the feminist in me want to scream and hit him and tell him I couldn't be claimed. But the fact was, he'd done it. He'd claimed me, repeatedly, last night. The best sex of my life, hands down. Hudson could win an award for pleasure. I just didn't want to think about how much practice that must have taken on people who were not me to get there.

"You're overthinking, precious," he mumbled against my lips, closing our kiss with soft little nips.

"It's kinda my thing." I frowned, collapsing into his arms and letting him take the load off my shoulders. Maybe I had issues with control now and again, and maybe someone like Hudson was the perfect antidote. Maybe taking this ride with him would help loosen me up. At least I knew there would be no heavy commitment at the end of it. Just the way Hudson talked, I could tell he wasn't the commitment type, so maybe he was my safe escape. My foray into reckless danger, and there was no way he could burn me because we were just a fling. This was just a fling, right? I was personally sure this was just a fling.

"Enough of the thinking. You should try feeling." His hands slipped down my torso and over the curve of my ass, pulling me against his straining erection. "This is anything but a fling to me, Skylar. The sooner you know that, the sooner we can get to the good stuff."

Oh God. This man was calling me on every single hang-up I had.

"Look, I know last night was incredible…" I emphasized the word—it was that incredible. "But we both have lives. I can't just upend everything for—"

"Oh, I see what's going on here." He patted my ass cheek. "You're only spontaneous with a little Scotch in your system." He winked.

"What?" I narrowed my eyes. "No, I'm just cautious."

"Boring." He arched an eyebrow.

"I prefer to think before I act."

"Predictable."

My cheeks flamed with anger. "And I don't normally fuck strangers."

His eyebrows shot up, that word eliciting the shock from him I'd wanted. "But…" His fingers slid between the cheeks of my ass, hovering so close I was preparing myself for his intrusion. "Best fuck of your life, right?"

My mouth popped open just as his finger made contact with the little rosebud of my ass, swirling and stretching until the tip was breaching me. "Oh God."

He didn't reply, only worked his finger against my asshole, sinking it a little deeper before I was full and overtaken by need, completely aching and desperate for more. Desperate for anything.

"I dare you to tell me it wasn't the best, Skylar." His other hand was working at the wet flesh of my pussy. "Because last night was fucking mind-blowing for me, and I know I'm not the only one who felt it. That pussy of yours was gushing like goddamn Niagara Falls. Your lips may be able to deny it, but that sweet, juicy cunt of yours was begging for my cock. You loved how full it felt with me inside you."

"No, I mean, yes." I shook my head, trying to maintain some sense of logic through the haze of him. "But that doesn't mean—"

"Like hell it doesn't, precious. I've never been with a woman like we were last night. You're another level, and I'm not a man who walks away from something so perfect sitting right in his lap."

He hoisted me against him then, hauling me into the shower and smothering my lips in a kiss. He flipped on the water with one hand, the other bending me over and then covering my palms with his own against the cool tile.

"Spread your thighs." His voice rumbled through my veins. He pushed my legs apart with his knees, his heavy palms sliding down my torso and rippling through my bloodstream. "Keep that pussy open for me, gorgeous."

His palm landed one swift crack between my thighs, his hand gone as quickly as it'd come, leaving a sting that charged through every nerve. My pussy dripped, my clit on fire with need for another orgasm. He landed another fast smack, then two more in quick succession before he was cupping me, swirling the rough pads of his fingers at my clit.

"So desperate for me you're burning up. This sweet cunt is so hot for me." One long finger slid deep inside, my body convulsing in waves, my vision blinded. "Where do you want my cock, pretty girl?"

"Inside me." I rasped. "I want you deep inside me."

"I was thinking…" His thumb slipped between my ass cheeks, pressing at the tight bud. "…here."

He spread the mixture of water and arousal around my ass, pressing the tip of his finger in slowly, working the muscle loose and making me groan and sigh in equal parts pleasure and pain.

"You like it when I'm a little dirty. I can feel how hot my finger up your tight ass makes you. You gush, baby. Your pussy drips that sweet juice for me. You begged for me to slap that cunt of yours. You kept arching up to meet my hand. You want to be filthy with me, sweet girl. I want you to know that everything is okay with me. All your desires, all your fantasies. I want you to have all the pleasure known to man. I want you to come for me, I want to drink from you until I am drunk with desire. It's all for you, baby."

I nodded, unable to form words. Feeling…I could only feel.

"You want my fat cock to fill this tight little asshole of yours?" He worked his finger a little deeper, my sighs growing to frantic pants as an orgasm burned just at the edge, just out of reach…

"Yes, oh my God, yes, I want more of you, Hudson."

"Fuck, that's what I need to hear, baby." He pulled his hand from my ass and pushed his fingers into my hair, turning my head to meet his lips for a hungry kiss. His dick nudged at my back entrance, the tip pushing at the edges, the only words running through my head: *please, more, Hudson.* "I want you so full you cream all over and then beg me for more, Sky. I want to mark you with my come. You would look so pretty covered in it. Your ass feels so good, baby. I love that you let me fuck you here. I want you to tell me how much you love this. I want you to be my dirty little girl."

Oh God, what would that piercing feel like buried in my ass? In the next instant, he was shoving into me, the fullness his cock created sending stars racing into my vision. He was buried inside me up to the tip, my fingers clutching at wet tile as a thousand pricks of delicious pain raced through me.

Thank God he'd prepped me with his finger, so the pain was only enough to cause a bite, followed by a surprising surge of pleasure. With every thrust, the pain of his intrusion melted deeper into pleasure. Our lips still attached, his hand still fucking perfect figure eights around my pussy, my orgasm barreling to the finish line far too soon.

"Let go, Sky. Give it all to me," his husky voice whispered, sending sparks straight to my clit.

I clamped down on my bottom lip, the hot water of the shower pelting my back and adding to all the sensations flooding my body. His hips worked against my ass, hand dancing across my flesh, lips planting kisses across my neck… I fell off the edge entirely.

Every passionate moment we'd had before now combined into a raging inferno of feeling that tsunamied through me, spinning my insides and lighting fire to every raw nerve.

"Fuck, that's the hottest thing I've ever seen." His teeth caught my ear. "You just squirted all over my hand."

My heart hammered as the realization flooded me. That orgasm had been different than any other; that orgasm had felt like something was ripping me apart from the inside and bursting into a thousand fireworks in every direction.

"That was incredible," I finally gasped out.

"You. Are. Incredible." His thrusts sped up, his hands fisting at both of my hips as he fucked me deeper, harder, beyond the edge of reason.

He was perfect…we were perfect.

He read my body, teased the pleasure from me. I couldn't get enough. And he couldn't get enough of me.

I'd never been so consumed, so hollowed out and filled up with another soul like I was when I was connected with him like his. Writhing together, we lost ourselves and then found each other again, new, whole, different, and so sated.

His hands raked across my body, bruised my skin as we fucked. He drove on until I was close to losing control again, too far gone to care, too lost to want to be found. The spray of hot water beat down on both of us as another orgasm orchestrated by him quaked through me. My muscles went lax, my heart thudding a tattoo against my ribs. Hudson fucked me senseless, and it seemed like every fuck was the best fuck of my life with him.

I watched rapt as his jaw went taut, his hands clutching at my ass as an orgasm tore through him. His face contorted with rabid pleasure, his lips suddenly sucking at my skin as he fucked the last remaining ounces of his release into my body.

Slathered against him, water, sweat, sex, and semen swirling down the drain, I felt tears prick my eyelids as I realized this was it.

I was lost.

There would be no coming back from Hudson.

Not ever again.

He dragged out of me, scraping against every naked nerve and pulling another raw sigh from my lips. His palm worked back and forth at my wet pussy, swirling our mixed juices, before both of his hands trailed up my body, two fingers swirling inside my mouth.

"Suck." He ordered, and if it weren't for his hand at my waist holding me to him, I would have fallen at his feet.

I sucked slowly, savoring the flavor of him and I mixed together.

"You're so beautiful, Skylar." He cupped my face, pressing his lips to mine and fucking me with his tongue, long and slow, making me weak all over again.

There would be no coming back from this man.

That was the moment Hudson ruined me.

Five

Hudson

Skylar spent the rest of the day curled up in my arms as we alternated between fucking, eating, talking, and fucking all over again.

Every hour that passed I learned more about her. And the longer we spent together, the more I found myself opening up to her in ways I never had with any other human.

Skylar made some of my sharp edges soft.

I couldn't explain it, didn't even give a shit about trying because I liked being with her so fucking much that nothing else mattered. If being buried inside her precious pussy made me the world's biggest pussy, so be it. I didn't live for the regrettable moments; I lived for the unforgettable ones, and Skylar had fast become a woman I couldn't see past.

My vision was blinded by her, and just the thought of going back to my real life felt like a sham because there was no real life without her in it.

I'd even found myself taking in her small, cozy home and imagining my stuff here, waking up to her in the mornings and putting her to bed at night in my arms.

I could see it, and I wanted it.

Moving my custom paint business up north wouldn't be such a big deal. I had clients traveling for hundreds of miles to bring me their bikes as it was. A few hours north wouldn't stop them.

By the time I realized I had somewhere to be tonight, I was already buried deep inside her, coaxing a third orgasm from her body when my eyes landed on the digital clock by her bed.

Fuck.

The wedding.

I'd have to leave her tonight, at least for a few hours.

Christ, I wished I could bail on that whole shitshow.

When soft mewls fell from Skylar's lips, I knew I'd done my job, the soft fluttering of her sweet cunt around my fingers driving me a little madder for her. "I could stay buried in your pussy all day and never come up for air."

I cupped her cheek, planting a soft kiss on the seam of her lips. She sighed, rocking against me, her hands working through my hair as she lay underneath me.

"I hate to say it, precious, but I've got to be somewhere for a few hours tonight. Whole reason I came up here, but then I found you and got a little distracted."

She smiled, stretching and arching, her pert little nipples pebbling in the warm sunlight. "I've got a thing too. I wish I could get out of it."

I plucked at her nipple with my fingertips, enjoying the soft squeal that escaped past her lips. "So, meet back here later?"

Her smile widened, one finger reaching out to trace the swell of my lips. "Until later, Hudson."

A groan rumbled from my chest as I rolled on top of

her, fusing our lips and wishing like hell I'd never have to leave her again.

"But first I need to fuck you with my tongue." I nudged her legs apart with my knees. "Coat my face in your juices so every man in a five-foot radius can smell your gorgeous cunt on me tonight."

* * *

I tapped my thumb on the edge of the linen-covered table, anxious as hell to get out of this place, ditch the aunts and uncles that were constantly complaining they didn't see me enough, and head right back to Sky's place. I couldn't keep my mind off her, images of last night rolling through my brain like a newsreel. Shaking my soon-to-be new stepfather's hand while remembering the silky skin between her thighs, making conversation with my mother as she fussed over where I'd been last night, I couldn't handle any of it. Everything was so damn mundane compared to the feelings I had when Skylar and I were together. I'd already decided I was ditching this rehearsal party early. Mom and Mark didn't even need a goddamn rehearsal; they'd both been there, done that. Several times.

Talk about dysfunction, I didn't even know why I was sitting here at the moment when I could be chasing something that really fucking mattered, could lead somewhere truly special. Suddenly feeling antsy, I rose from my chair, taking long strides to the bar to order another whiskey. The moments spent without Sky took too damn long as far as I was concerned. I hoped the booze would help speed time.

I tossed a few dollars' tip into the jar, taking a slow sip when my eyes landed on an auburn-haired beauty across the room. The soft, slinky dress she wore left little to the imagination, and I could see all the sexy contours that woman possessed.

I launched across the room on determined strides, my cock already searing the back of my zipper as my eyes roamed up and down her form. She was just approaching what I assumed was her chair when I reached her.

"Didn't expect later to come so soon," I cooed at her ear, hooking her elbow with mine and hauling her against me.

"Hudson." Her hands pressed against the solid wall of my chest. "What are you doing?"

"I need a minute." My eyes slammed into hers, pulling her a little tighter against me so she could feel just what being with her did to me. It was an instant reaction, our bodies in tune. Even from across the room, I'd been drawn to her like a moth to a flame.

"Okay," she said breathily, eyes still focused on mine.

I threaded our fingers together and led her out of the crowded room and down a long corridor. I shoved through the first exit door we came across, crisp air hitting our faces and, in my case, fulfilling the lust. "What the hell are you wearing?"

"What are you talking about?" She cocked her head to the side and inched away from me.

"This?" I plucked at the thin spaghetti strap, barely holding in the heavy weight of her tits. My tits. Mine. "I can see every dip and curve of your body."

"It's the only thing that fit," she replied, crossing her arms, her tits pressing together and bursting out of what was otherwise a modest neckline.

"Christ, you were put on this earth to kill me, weren't you?" I shrugged out of my coat, putting it over her shoulders and leading her a few steps around the corner of the building so we were completely out of sight of the parking lot. "I would have taken you shopping today. All you had to do was say something."

"Well, I was a little preoccupied. What are you doing here?"

"I was thinking about you all warm and cozy in your bed until I looked across the room and saw you—and not only saw you, but saw you wearing this." I leaned in, my breath washing across her neck. "What, do you want every man in that room to know what you look like naked?" Her nipples puckered under the silky fabric. "Mmm." I plucked at the little nub, enjoying the shudder I elicited. "You do. You're a kinky little thing, aren't you?"

My hands slipped down her body, pulling up the silky fabric before my fingertips met heaven.

"I can't stop replaying last night. The memory of being lost inside you is haunting me."

Her hands clutched at my shoulder blades. "Oh God, me too."

"I can't fucking think straight when you're in the room, and hell if I want to, Sky." My lips attached to hers, fingers fumbling at the zipper on my pants before her little hand was fisted around my cock, her thumb working over the pierced ridge and sending bullets of arousal through my veins. In the next instant, she was guiding me into her hot body. I cradled her against the wall, her heels digging into my ass as I slammed into her so hard my eyes nearly rolled back in my head. Everything about the way we connected was intense and all-consuming.

"Oh, Hudson," she whispered against my neck.

"God…"

My hand tightened at her waist, my hips hitting a new position and sending her shuddering and shattering around me. "Fuck, love the feel of you milking my cock, precious. Can't even think straight around you."

Watching those ragged little pants wash over her lips, feeling the way her nails dug into my skin and left marks, the pleasure and pain sensation pounded through me. It battered my body until I was emptying every ounce of passion I had in me into her, long and hard. I wanted us fucking melded, bonded, tied in every sense of the word. I had to keep her, had to protect her, had to love her.

Everything about her, I loved, from the flaming red hair to the fiery temper that matched it. This woman was made just for me, and not a thing could tear us apart. "We need to get home."

"Yeah," she sighed, chest still heaving.

I smiled deeply, pulling myself out of her body and tucking my dick back in my pants. I straightened her dress, sliding the silk down her thighs and rearranging her hair so she did not look just freshly fucked. As much as I loved that look on her, it wasn't any other goddamn person's business. "You're never allowed to leave the house in this dress again."

She rolled her eyes before a slow grin curved her lips. "Thanks for rescuing me. That was way more fun."

"Happy to be at your service anytime, precious." I hooked her hand in mine and walked us back to the door, opening it for her and letting her walk in ahead of me. She spun, a beautiful smile splitting her face, and she was about to open her mouth to say something before someone else cut in.

"Skylar! I've been looking for you—oh." Mark, my

mother's soon-to-be husband appeared from behind her. "I see you've met Darcy's son. We were hoping to introduce you officially, but looks like you've beaten me to it. Darcy?" Mark looked over his shoulder before my mother appeared behind him.

"Oh, hi, honey! I was looking for you. I wanted to introduce you to your new stepsister, but I guess you've already found her. Skylar and I met for the first time tonight. Isn't she just the prettiest thing?" My mother's eyes gleamed back at me.

Fuck. My. Life.

Six

Skylar

"Skylar, this is Hudson, Darcy's son." My father's words ran like a speeding train through my head.

How had this happened?

Why was God punishing me?

I was pretty sure I was being punished for something at this point.

How was it possible that the man I'd been sleeping with, the man who'd given me the very best orgasms of my life, was actually my new stepbrother. Clearly, God had one helluva sense of humor, and right now, his attention was aimed at me.

"So, did you just meet here, or…?" Hudson's mom asked politely, eyes circling from her son to me and back again. I frowned, thinking there was no way out of this one, before Hudson saved me.

"Met up last night, actually, in town at one of the local watering holes."

"Ah, so that's where you were last night." Darcy smiled, before realization seemed to dawn and her eyes grew wide as dinner plates. "Um, Mark, honey, can I have a word with you?" She hooked my father's hand in hers then hauled him down the hallway and out of view.

"Fuck." Hudson shot a hand through his hair, eyes turning to me. "Didn't see that one coming."

I stood speechless, the last few terrifying minutes cycling in my head. "I don't even know what to say."

Hudson's grin split a little wider, his hand locking with mine and pulling me against his body. "Fucking your stepbrother now—I knew you liked it kinky."

My mouth shot open, horror and anger and every other conflicting emotion playing on my face. "That's not true! What—" I huffed, frustration dripping out of every pore. "You're incredible."

"You already told me that last night." He nuzzled into my neck, tongue darting out to lick along the crease.

"Stop, now is definitely not the place—"

"Overthinking again." He covered my mouth with his in a deep kiss, shutting me up and turning me to putty in the same instant. Hudson had a superpower, I was sure of it. "I think we've done our due diligence. I need you alone now." He took my hand and hauled me right back out of the door we'd come in, striding to his bike, which, funnily enough, was parked only a few spots away from my car. We'd missed each other earlier by just a few tick marks, but we had each other now, and if his grip was any indication, he wouldn't be letting go.

"Leave the car here. I'm thinking we've both got the same thing we've got to be at tomorrow, so I'll bring you."

"Bring me?" I gasped as he hauled me onto his bike. "Is that…allowed?"

"A man can bring his little step-sis to the wedding, right? I'm pretty sure that makes me a gentleman."

"Oh my God, there aren't even any words to describe

how vile you are."

"The way you scream my name when my head is between your thighs is a good start." He revved the engine to life with a wink.

"I don't know if I'm making the best decision of my life or the worst going home with you right now."

"Got news for you, precious. The time for decisions was last night. Today, you're all mine. Tomorrow too. There's no turning this train around. You're stuck with me."

I huffed out a breath, enjoying the feeling of butterflies battering my insides at his words. "Looks like I'm stuck with you even more than I realized."

"Ain't that the truth." He grinned that crooked grin, eyes sparkling before he tore out of the parking lot and down the street, aiming straight for my house. He'd already weaseled his way into my heart; so what if our parents had just dropped a bomb? I was living recklessly, feeling and not thinking, and we weren't related anyway, so it's not like there was anything awkward about it.

Or there shouldn't be.

Until I thought of Christmas dinners and summer barbecues and what would happen if Hudson and I didn't work out. What if he was a raging lunatic asshole who was going to trample all over my heart and leave it bleeding in the dust?

I gripped at his waist, holding on a little tighter, before he took one hand off the handlebars and covered mine.

Just that small touch had my body loosening, my anxiety easing, and the sense that this was right -- and so was he -- growing strong again.

We'd face tomorrow however it needed facing. But right now, it was just him and me on the back of his bike, and I kind of loved it.

* * *

Later that night, long after the shock had worn off—and Hudson had given me four mind-bending orgasms—I burrowed into the haven of his arms, a sense of dread taking root in my belly. "Tomorrow is the wedding."

"Yup," he breathed, fingertips tracing circles around my nipple.

"Tomorrow, you leave?"

"Yeah." The word escaped his lips on a soft puff of air.

"I hate tomorrow already."

"Me too." The words stretched between us, unspoken thoughts hanging heavy. "Being lost in you is something spiritual, Sky. I'm not the same man when I'm with you. I'm better." His words were like a wringer to my heart. How had we found ourselves here? Riding the impossible high of stolen first moments right into the inevitable crash and burn of impossible love. "I never saw you coming, precious. You completely blindsided me."

I curled into his body, unable to take the loss of this man just yet. Tears pricked at my eyelids as he tucked me under his heavy arm, stroking my hair with his callused fingers and whispering sweet nothings in my ear. Everything he did was meant to make me feel better, but somehow it made it worse. It made everything worse because tomorrow he was leaving, and the simple fact was we should just go back to our real lives and forget this ever happened. Now more than ever.

We couldn't show up to family gatherings hand in hand. We couldn't live under the guise of love when so much dysfunction surrounded our coupling.

I stroked his chest, wishing more than anything that today hadn't happened so we could go back to just being us, Skylar and Hudson, two strangers who met in a bar and fucked one night.

But we would never just be that anymore. We were now the stepsiblings who'd fucked, who'd filled in all the missing pieces, who loved each other? Was that true? Did he love me? Because I was starting to think I could love him, just when it was all being stolen away.

"Penny for your thoughts?"

"Just overthinking again," I muttered, trying to control the cracks from shattering my voice.

"We've got to train that out of you," he whispered softly, emotion flowing through his words as much as mine.

"Yeah." I frowned, trying desperately not to crumble in his arms.

"Sky?" he murmured against my skin.

"Yeah?"

His fingers laced with mine as he took his time replying. "I love you more than I thought I could ever love anyone. I just want you to know that."

My throat ached with the lump I was trying to squash, until finally the levees burst, and I let a few stubborn tears trickle down my cheeks. I tried to hide it, but I didn't do a very good job when the salty wetness on his chest drew his attention to my face.

He pulled me closer, hands in my hair as he kissed away the trails of tears.

Hudson had turned my world upside down then soothed away the tight feeling that clenched my heart whenever I thought of him leaving. He knew my soul inside and out, and letting go of him tomorrow would be the hardest thing I'd ever have to do.

Seven

Skylar

"I guess I didn't think very far ahead last night when we left. This dress on the back of your bike is going to be a challenge." I frowned, glancing at the seat of his bike then down to my full-length gown.

He smiled, helping me onto the back of the bike. "I've got you, precious."

He tucked me sideways on his lap, holding me nestled in his strong thighs, one arm looped around my waist as he fired up the engine.

"I'm pretty sure this isn't safe." I loved him pressed to me, the smell of his skin intoxicating, the feel of his broad form against mine making me lose my senses a little more.

"Remember what I told you the first night?"

I shook my head, struggling to remember so many of the things. My brain had been in full meltdown mode once his touch heated all of my nerves.

"I said I'd rather die than let anything happen to you." His eyes nailed mine for a moment. "I meant it, Sky. I meant every word I said this weekend. You've just got to give me the go-ahead, because I'm all in."

He swept the air from my lungs as he eased slowly into the parking lot, which was already filling up with rows of cars.

"I don't think we can."

"We can do anything, precious. Life is ours for the taking."

"You say that like it's so simple, so easy."

"It is when you know something is right. I'm a guy who lives by his instincts. If it doesn't feel right, I don't do it. But this…" His palm tightened at my knee. "Everything about you feels right."

"What, are you going to move up here? I just can't up and leave everything—"

"I would, for you." The bike pulled to a slow stop, his eyes hovering over mine as we shared a thousand unspoken words.

"I can't ask that of you. I'm sorry, Hudson, but I think we just chalk this up to—"

"What? To a one-night stand? To a fling? I told you, it was never that for me, and it's the furthest thing from it now. I love you, Sky, and I can't just turn that off."

"I know, I know, I…" My heart nearly cracked open. "I love you too, but—"

"But shit." His face hardened, and he pulled me from the bike, setting me on my feet and straightening my dress for me. "The big moment's about to start. We should get in there." He was effectively shutting me down. I'd hurt him. Somehow, I'd hurt this strong, stubborn, maddening man. What had my life become?

We walked side by side, Hudson's hand noticeably absent from my own as we walked into the garden my father and Hudson's mother had chosen to be married in. We trekked down the aisle, splitting when the usher escorted me to the groom's side, Hudson to the bride's side.

A thousand pounds of cement crashed down on my chest then, making it hard to breathe as I settled in my seat and tried to focus on the next few minutes. I swiped at the screen of my phone, fighting the tears from my eyes as I sat still, waiting for this goddamn wedding to start so that it would be over and I could get the hell out of here.

My phone vibrated with a message, an unknown number popping up on my screen.

"Weddings are for happy tears, not sad ones."

I smiled, sniffing before I typed back. **"Are you just staring at me from over there?"**

"You're the most beautiful girl in the room, how could I not?" Came his instant reply.

Fingers of love unfurled in my stomach as I wished he were sitting right beside me now. To hell with what anyone else thought; he made me feel better, and that's all that mattered.

"You're a charmer."

"So that explains why your stepbrother found his way into your pants this weekend. ;)"

I nearly choked on my tongue with his last text. I shot a glare over the crowd at him, and he shrugged, that cocky grin deepening on his face.

"I don't know if I hate you or love you."

"Acting like stepsiblings already."

"Hudson!" I typed out fiercely, my heart thundering as an amused grin finally spread its way across my face.

"What? Made you smile, didn't I?"

I turned, sending him one long look before his grin cracked open and he chuckled loudly. A few of the people sitting around him cast him a glance before he shrugged and waggled his eyebrows at me.

God, I loved that man.

Damn me to hell if it was wrong, but the way he lit me up could not be denied.

The music started then, and I made a point of tucking my phone into my purse so he knew I was onto his games and he couldn't fuck with me through the whole ceremony. Even if the ceremony would be a whole lot more interesting if he did.

My father made his way down the aisle, pausing to wink once at me before stopping at the altar. He was such a sweet old guy, and when my mom had up and left him for another man when I was three, he hadn't batted an eye, only went on raising me the best he knew how. He even jumped into a half-assed marriage with a woman when I was a teenager under his sweet but misguided assumption that I needed a mother figure. I think she and I fought more than the two of them did. Thankfully, that marriage didn't last long; within six months she was talking to a divorce lawyer. It was good to have my dad back, and it wasn't long after that he began grooming me to run his accounting business alongside him, and I liked it. And while maybe it wasn't my dream job, it kept me happy and kept a roof over my head, so I was thankful for all the things he'd given me.

I didn't know anything about Hudson's mom, but if she raised a son like Hudson, then I had to have hope she was a good woman who would be there for my dad. If Hudson had gotten any of his loyalty and protectiveness from his mom, then I had a feeling my dad would be A-OK.

By the time the bride and groom were finally kissing, I

was swiping at happy tears and lost in the moment of love with them. As the music kicked up once again, they walked back down the aisle hand in hand, deliriously happy grins plastered onto their faces. I clapped and cheered for them, putting aside my helpless feeling only for a beat to share in their moment.

As the crowd flooded down the aisle after the happy couple, Hudson found me in the chaos and threaded his fingers with mine. "That was the longest thirty minutes of my life."

"Oh, look how happy they are. It's good."

"I was only watching you. Every emotion that crossed your face as you watched them nearly undid me, Sky."

He paused, stilling where I stood and leaving us alone as the crowd moved to the tents set up for the reception.

"Why do you keep saying these things? You're making it harder, Hudson," I nearly sobbed, finally cracking from the pressure.

"Because I say what I mean, Skylar. Always have and always will."

I frowned, appreciating his honesty, even though his words were like an arrow through my heart.

"We've got a party to get to. I've only got a few more hours with my favorite girl. I want to spend them wisely." His eyes shimmered down at me, seeing straight into my soul.

I nodded, letting our hands tangle as we walked across the lawn to the covered tables. Just before we reached the tent, he angled me around the corner. "Where are we going?"

"Need a minute alone with you if I'm going to get through this night."

Warmth curled through my stomach with his words.

As soon as we turned the corner, his hands were at my waist, his lips attaching to mine in a desperate kiss. His heavy cock pressed between us, the memory of that pierced wonder sliding in and out of me sending shockwaves through my pussy.

"I want to taste you."

"What?" he murmured against my lips.

"I want you in my mouth, Hudson."

"Sky—" I cut him off when I dropped to my knees, hands working at the zipper on his pants. "Fuck. If you wanted to suck my dick, precious, all you had to do was ask." His stormy eyes peered down at me, both of his hands working into my hair and tightening. "Tell me what you want."

"I want to suck you off." Embarrassment colored my cheeks, arousal flaming between my thighs. He arched one eyebrow, stroking my cheek tenderly, waiting for more. "Please, I want to swallow your dick, Hudson."

"Good girl." He pulled the zipper down on his pants and fisted his cock at the root. Just the vision of him, broad and powerful, standing with his dick in his hand and waiting for me to suck him off was powerful. I wanted to be good enough for him. I wanted to bring him to his knees.

"Use your tongue," he growled, the tip already glistening with a bead of precome.

I cupped his heavy balls in my palm, enjoying the shudder that came from somewhere above me before I stroked the tip of my tongue up the silky skin of his shaft. His hips jerked, small grunts on his lips as I ran my tongue along the ridge and caught the barbell with my tongue. He grunted when I tugged on it softly with my teeth before swallowing him completely, forcing the tip of his thick dick down my throat.

His hands tightened in my hair before I sucked up the length again, my thighs shifting back and forth as his hips jerked, his cock twitching as I sucked and swallowed.

"Christ, Sky, I won't last long if you keep doing that." He growled, pulling me up to his lips and tangling our tongues together. "You're too beautiful to be on your knees anyway."

He dropped to his knees then shoved my silky dress over my thighs. His hand slid against my wet pussy, swirling my arousal before his tongue lapped up my drenched seam. I sighed, hands digging into his hair for support. He wrapped one of my knees around his neck, allowing me to lean into him as he sucked and hummed at my clit.

One of his hands disappeared from my thigh and fisted at his cock then, jerking it quickly as he fucked me with his tongue, his teeth nipping, his lips sucking.

Jesus, he was…

This was…

"Oh my God." I breathed as my thighs began a slow shake. His hand moved quicker around his cock as he jerked it between my legs, his lips sucking fiercely just as announcements for the bride and groom started in the tent not even a hundred yards from where he was eating me.

"Gush for me, baby. Cover me in your sweet cream." His teeth sank into my flesh, and an orgasm burned through my body, shaking my legs, loosening every muscle, and sending me into another world.

Hudson's soft grunts and the warmth coating my cunt told me he was coming with me. Our orgasms mixing, our pleasure overwhelming, our love binding.

"Fuck, you're all I need, Sky." His words struck a chord deep inside me, the need to feel him, connect with him, love him stronger than it had been in all the moments leading up to now.

"Kiss me," I whispered, not sure what else to say.

He straightened my dress then tucked his cock into his pants before standing and pulling me against his heavy chest. Our lips connected, soft and slow, but the kiss still dark in its intensity.

Enveloped in him, I found my happy place.

"I'm tempted to kidnap you."

"I'm tempted to let you." I smiled.

"Don't tease me."

"Where would the fun be in that?" I winked. "How long we talkin'?"

He sucked in a slow breath, pressing another kiss to my lips before answering. "Forever."

His words singed a permanent path to my heart. "I wish forever was that simple."

"Maybe it is." He locked his hand in mine, throwing me a reckless smile as he led us back toward the tent.

"Nothing ever is."

"I beg to differ."

"Of course you do." I sighed, unable to shake the feeling of doom.

We turned the corner then, slipping into the tent and settling at a table in the back that had empty chairs.

Within minutes, his fingertips were hovering at my knee, tracing up the soft skin of my thighs and turning my stomach to churned butter. After light appetizers and aperitifs were served, none of which I was able to stomach because his nearness was intoxicating enough on its own, the DJ started playing old-fashioned Sinatra tunes.

The opening lines of "Strangers in the Night" started, and I smiled. "This is my favorite Sinatra song. My dad always used to sing it to me before bed. A weird choice, I know, but I always looked forward to it."

"Well, then I'd like to have this dance." He pulled me from my chair, locking our hands and guiding me to the dance floor already studded with romantic couples.

"Are you sure?" My eyes darted around the space, hoping my father wouldn't notice us dancing. But then again, what was so wrong with two people dancing?

"I'm more sure of you than I've ever been, Skylar." He said the words so matter-of-factly it nearly made me stumble.

He caught me before I went careening into him, his hands at my waist and his lips at my ear. "You look so beautiful today," he whispered, moving us back and forth to the soft crooning music. "Made me think of what kind of bride you'll be." His words coiled through my insides like snakes. "That'll be you up there someday, Sky."

I sucked in a lungful of breath, the unspoken meaning of his words clear. Someday, I would be up there, but it wouldn't be with him. It could never be with him.

I couldn't do this anymore—the passion, the emotion, the separation too much to bear.

I clenched my teeth, no longer able to enjoy the feel of him against me when I knew he'd be leaving within the hour, heading south and far away from me.

"I'm sorry. I can't." I choked up and dashed out of his arms, running for the exit.

Eight

Hudson

I charged out of the doors after her, the only thing running through my head: catch her.

I couldn't let her get away; I couldn't let this be our last moment. We'd shared too much, felt too much, loved too much.

If I could cut and run on the business and move up here to shack up with her tomorrow, I would. But it wasn't that simple.

I'd had the custom paint shop for almost a decade now, and business was better than ever. It'd take me at least a few months to close things out in the city, get a place rented or purchased up here, and have everything moved. Just thinking about it made my chest ache.

I caught sight of her, waves of auburn hair whipping in the wind as she sped to her car.

Fuck.

I ran full tilt after her, catching her only when she had a hand on the door and was ready to climb in.

"Fuck, you run fast in those heels." I sucked in a breath of air.

"It's a talent. I'm going to go home. I'm sorry, it's just

best if we let this end…"

I swallowed the baseball lodged in my throat, fingers tightening on her elbow as I pulled us together. "Don't say that."

"I can't figure out how to do this. Did you see the looks my dad was giving me? I thought he was going to have a coronary, I'm sorry, but for them, we can't do this."

"For them? For them! What about us, Sky? What about the fact that you make me feel happier than I've ever been, that you make me feel alive for the first time? My mom spent my whole life dragging me around from husband to husband. I don't have much faith in relationships, and frankly, never have, but you and I are different. It didn't take me long to see that at all."

"I know, but, Hudson, it will crush them. My dad has spent his whole life building a business, building a reputation in this community—"

"And you think we ruin that?" He laughed, a hard edge to his words.

"No, but…I don't know." I finally gave in, realizing that was the whole problem with this scenario; I didn't know what the future held.

"I won't beg you to love me, Skylar." He shook his head, eyes holding mine as they shimmered with emotion. "You've got my number. I hope you use it."

My heart thundered, my palms sweating, and tears burned trails down my cheeks as I watched him walk away.

But I stood rooted, speechless, knowing it was the best thing.

I couldn't break my daddy's heart. I was his only daughter; he wanted to walk me down the aisle someday

—and not to give me away to my stepbrother.

Hudson slung one leg over his Harley, the contrast of the handsome guy in the sharp suit on the big bike just one of the contradictions I'd come to love about him. The gauge in his ear was the only outward indication he didn't quite fit in with these people. Hudson had edge, I never knew what would come out of his mouth, and he lived his life unapologetically. No regret, no shame, just feeling.

I sucked in a ragged breath, turning my head away when his bike roared to life.

I clutched at the door of my car, willing myself to get in, my heart begging me to take one last look. Just one final look at the man who had altered the very course of my life.

The bike paused as he waited at the exit, the slow, steady rumble vibrating through the asphalt and straight into my heart.

"Wait," I whispered, my voice cracking. "I love you."

As if he'd heard me, though it was impossible that he could have, he turned his head, eyes locking with mine one last time as I mouthed the words to him again, "I love you," and I swiped at another stubborn tear.

His head angled down, then away, before I did the same, turning my back on the man who'd rocked my very foundations. The engine roared, and just when I was expecting the sound to fade, it grew stronger until it was vibrating through the soles of my feet again.

I glanced up, finding he was riding straight for me, a determined look in his eye.

He was coming for me.

"Hop on, precious. I'm not leaving this town without you on the back of my bike. I'm making an executive decision on this one." His crooked grin stole my heart.

"Good." Fresh tears rolled down my cheeks as I launched myself at him. He caught me in his firm embrace, lips bonding to mine as we kissed until we couldn't breathe. Kissed like we'd never been kissed. Kissed like it was our very last moment together on earth.

But it wasn't.

It so wasn't.

"Told ya you're stuck with me, Sky. Hope you're ready for that."

"Bring it, Hudson." I grinned up at him when he pulled me onto his lap, sandwiching me between his heavy body and the handlebars and tipping me back, my hair cascading in long waves off the side of his bike. His lips fastened to my throat, working up the column of my neck before landing at my lips and kissing me completely breathless.

"I'm finally ready," I announced, eyes unwavering as I held his.

"Took you long enough. I've been ready since the second you started flirting with me at that bar."

"Me?" I giggled, circling my hands around his neck. "You were doing the flirting."

He shrugged, revving the engine again. "Ready for forever, precious?"

"Only if you're in it."

"You'd better believe it. You're not getting rid of me, no matter how hard you try."

"Well, I'm done trying."

"Just feeling?"

"Just feeling," I confirmed. "Someone once said I think too much. So I'm trying it his way for a while."

"I like the sound of that." His hand wrapped around my waist as we pulled out of the parking lot again, this time headed south.

I didn't know what the next step would hold for us, but letting Hudson leave had become harder than staying alone without him. Fuck the status quo, I wanted the new, the reckless. I was all feeling, and for the first time in my life, I was listening to my heart—and I could hear what my heart was saying loud and clear.

Love Hudson with everything in you—because love like that doesn't come around very often.

There was no going back for us. We were only looking forward now.

Epilogue

Skylar - two years later

"Ready, precious?" Hudson's worlds curled my toes.

I snuggled my arms around his waist, breathing in his warm scent. "I don't think I'll ever be."

He grinned down at me, one arm wrapping around my shoulders and enveloping me. "I think this little man has something else to say about it." He grinned broadly as our son toddled a few steps closer to us, his chubby little body decked out in leather motorcycle boots, dark jeans, and a black onesie featuring a little skull wearing a bandanna across the forehead.

Hudson had picked up that little outfit in honor of our little man's first ride on the motorcycle with Daddy. Just around the yard, but still, it was a big moment.

"Don't you just want to snuggle with Mama on the porch and watch Daddy ride, Blake?" I scooped our darling little boy into my arms and smooched on his cheeks.

"He's done enough snuggling. This guy was born to ride." Hudson lifted Blake out of my arms, peppering him with kisses of his own. Seeing the two of them together was without a doubt the greatest gift I'd been given.

We'd both gotten the surprise of our life with this one. Just a few months after I left the wedding with Hudson, I'd missed my period, and in true Hudson form, he'd taken it all in stride. Shrugged and given me that devastatingly charming grin before hopping on his bike to go buy me a pregnancy test. We waited together in the tiny bathroom of my home, already overcrowded with all of his man-stuff. Then tears of complete joy had burned in my eyes when Hudson had held up the little white stick. Two pink lines.

If things with Hudson had been good before then, they were incredible after he found out I was carrying his baby. To say I was doted on for nine months straight was the understatement of the century. Hudson took care of the people he loved; he proved that to me and to Blake every single day.

"Ready to roll, big guy?" Hudson jostled Blake on his hip as our son reached out to the gleaming black Harley that was now a permanent fixture in my driveway. Ever since that kid could crawl, he was drawn to the big bike, and I couldn't blame him. I loved it too. It was the bike we'd shared our first kiss on and where we were the first moment Hudson's hands had caressed my skin. That bike was as much a part of our relationship as we were.

Hudson slung one leg over the bike, keeping our son firmly locked in one arm. The engine turned on, the soft purr coming to life as my son's eyes grew to the size of saucers. A huge grin followed, and if there'd been any doubt before now, it was obvious he was just like his daddy. I grinned proudly as Hudson slowly backed the bike out of the driveway, one eye on Blake's reaction the entire time.

He didn't have to worry; Blake was already shrieking and clapping with anticipation.

Once Hudson cleared the bumper of my car, he turned the handlebars and eased off into the grass of our front lawn. I laughed and waved at them as Blake's eyes followed me then whipped around to see where they were headed. Blake was the definition of joyful, and both of them were the definition of love. My heart was full to the brim with those two men. They would always have my heart, and there wasn't a day that went by when I wasn't thankful for them.

I glanced around, taking in my small house and reflecting on how my life had changed so much in two short years.

All of our firsts had happened here. So living here, bringing our son home to this house—something felt eternally right about it.

When I'd hopped on Hudson's bike with him and left the wedding, we'd only gone back to the city for a few days. I'd called out of work, and as soon as Hudson crossed the threshold of his spacious city-view apartment, he began the process of moving his entire business to my small hometown upstate.

There hadn't even been a decision to be made. He was sick of the city life, he said. He'd found everything he wanted in small-town living. He'd said his clients would follow him, and they had. And the entire move had seemed to work out for the better as he'd been able to find more space at a cheaper rent for his shop. Hudson had been able to use the extra income to hire a few more talented artists to take the custom paint business to another level.

And boy had he. The business was making so much

money at this point that he didn't even have to work as much. He was spending more and more time at home with Blake and me.

And that was a good thing, because our family was rapidly expanding.

After we'd found out Blake was coming, Hudson had dropped to one knee that very night, slipping an elegant ring on my finger that he'd already purchased. I loved wearing his ring. I loved being his. I even wanted to share his name, but before we could stop to plan a wedding, I was six months pregnant, and in no way did I want to stuff myself into a wedding dress. Hudson had crooned into my neck that he'd marry me naked, but I still wasn't ready.

And so we waited until our mini man was born. But raising the little guy was a full-time job. I struggled with recovering, feeling exhausted and run-down constantly, and so I'd kept pushing the wedding. Hudson was patient, as always. I think, in all reality, it didn't even matter to him because he knew I was his and he was mine. We belonged to each other, and to prove it, he'd already started wearing a simple titanium wedding band to match my engagement ring.

We were in love, we were a deliriously happy family, but the timing for a wedding still wasn't right. Maybe deep down we wondered what our wedding would look like. Would our families really come together to celebrate our engagement? Did it even matter what they thought? And did we really want them there?

My dad had always been incredibly accepting of Hudson and me, never once judging us or our decisions. But Hudson's mother held a different view. And so we carried on, happy to make no formal decision and just live and feel, moment to moment.

The subject had come up again this spring when I'd started to feel depleted, emotional, and then another missed period.

Our second baby was on the way, my belly protruding at this very moment, five months along as we waited for our family to expand. Hudson had bent down on his knee again that night, tears glimmering in his deep eyes as he cupped my belly with his large palms. "Marry me, precious. Take my name."

"I will," I'd sworn, stroking my fingers through his messy hair. "Not yet, but I promise, soon."

His lips had turned up, placing a delicate kiss on the center of my abdomen. "Stubborn woman."

I grinned, thinking if I had a penny for every time he'd said that over the last few years… "Think about it." He stood, and I wrapped my arms around him. "The kids will be old enough that they can be there and understand, share it with us."

"Hell if I'm waiting that long." He nipped at my lips, a growl vibrating from his throat.

"We've waited this long, Hudson. If we do it now, I want it to be perfect. And right now, I wouldn't feel perfect."

"You're always perfect, precious. Every day spent with you is more perfect than the last." His hands cupped my face, lips tracing the angles of my cheeks.

"I love you, Hudson."

"Love you back, Sky." His words lit trails of fire through my heart.

I heard the rev of the engine coming back around the house, smiling as the two men in my life appeared.

"How was it?" I grinned. "He looks happy."

Hudson pulled the bike to a stop, planting a kiss on our son's red head before setting him down on the grass. Blake immediately burst into tears and lifted his hands straight in the air, begging to be picked up by his daddy. "Guess he wants to go on."

"He's a daredevil. Runs in the blood, I think." I placed a kiss on Hudson's cheek. He pulled our son into his arms, cuddling him close and then pulling me into him, whispering an endless array of I love yous into my neck.

My life was full, my heart overflowed, all thanks to a stranger who'd stolen my heart and soul one unforgettable night.

Second Epilogue

Skylar - four years later

"I look fat." I pouted in the mirror.

"Shh." Hudson's hands circled my waist, nuzzling against my ear. "You look fucking delicious. I want to peel this frilly shit off you and taste you with my tongue."

"That's your dick talking. He doesn't get a vote."

My husband's laugh echoed around the penthouse suite he'd rented for us overlooking the city. "Like hell, he doesn't. He picked you, didn't he?"

I rolled my eyes then shifted subjects. "How do you think the kids are? Should we call them?"

"No way. You're all mine tonight. I'm sure they're being spoiled with ice cream and movies with Grandma right now."

I sighed, unable to help the worry from shooting through me. I'd quickly learned after having a baby that you were essentially carving your heart in pieces and giving it away to another human being, letting it walk around outside your body. "Do you think the boys are being nice to Claudia?"

"Boys always pick on their sisters, it's a thing. Look how I pick on you." He winked. "Kinky mama."

"I can't believe you won't let me live it down." The memory of the night we'd found out we were stepsiblings still came back to me. It wasn't such a big deal anymore, even Hudson's mom had grown to accept it and love us together, but I think the grandkids had more to do with that than anything else.

And now here we were, tied to each other in blood, and now finally in name.

We shared three gorgeous kids, Blake, Lawson, and Claudia, and we were all still packed like sardines into the house we'd been in since the beginning. I loved that place, but it was time to sell. Hudson had already purchased a large plot of land outside of town for us, and building was set to start on our new, stupidly spacious home the very next week.

Tomorrow morning, we were flying to Hawaii for our honeymoon, after our parents and children had attended a small ceremony on the rooftop of the highest building in the city. It was small, intimate, so perfect, and my dad was even able to walk me down the aisle, Blake and Lawson giggling behind him in their little man-suits. The most precious memory of my life would always be that one. Claudia had clapped happily on the sidelines in her frilly white dress. Tears had sparkled in my eyes as I exchanged vows to love and honor my husband, our children as witnesses.

It was the perfect wedding, the perfect moment, and now we were set to take off for the perfect honeymoon. It was just that I hadn't spent more than a single night away from them yet, so leaving for a week was like another form of torture.

"You're overthinking again, precious." Hudson's palms crawled up my legs under the silky fabric that fell in an

A-line down my hips.

"Mmm, I can't imagine what the cure for that is." I looped my hand around his neck, finally succumbing to the lure of the first few moments alone with my gorgeous husband.

"I can." He hummed, dropping to his knees and lifting my wedding gown over his head, slipping under and finding me bare underneath, just for him. "Jesus, Sky, what are you trying to do to me? If I would have known you didn't wear panties to our wedding...?"

I dissolved in a fit of giggles before he stroked on long delicious lick up the seam of my pussy. "Oh God."

"My favorite words," he mumbled against my clit, teeth clamping on and dragging, ricocheting a thousand bullets of arousal through my body. "I had no idea my stepsister's pussy could taste so sweet."

"Oh my God, Hudson." I swatted his head before he caught my wrist, sucking one finger into his mouth, his lips covered in my arousal. Tornadoes of lust swirled in my stomach as his tongue worked up and down my finger, teeth nipping at the tip before he ducked back under the dress, attacking my pussy with his tongue and fingers again.

I sighed and arched against the wall as his finger sank inside me, his tongue sucking and lapping at my hot flesh.

"Fuck, you're amazing, Hudson. Completely amazing."

"Don't forget it, Skylar Farrow." His name married with mine was so erotic, my release passed the point of no return. My thighs began to shake, my fingers tugging at his hair as he continued his assault on my cunt. "Feels really fucking good to give you my name."

He sank another finger into me, and I splintered in a dozen different directions, my heart sliced into shards as I came apart under his hands.

I loved this man, loved him against all my better judgment, against the wishes of everyone we knew, and it was the very best thing that could have ever happened to me.

Hudson and I were only strangers in the night, but when I found him, I found my other half.

Hudson and Skylar Farrow.

It had a nice ring to it.

I grinned, Hudson sliding the dress up my body and depositing it in a heap on the floor before his lips attached to mine.

"You and those kids are the best things that have ever happened to me," he whispered, sending heat through my skin. "Even if we are kinda sorta related."

"Hudson!" I swatted his chest.

"Kiss me, *step-sis*. I need all of you tonight, and every other night of forever."

THE END

Turn the page to read the first three chapters of

Under Her Hood*!*

UNDER HER HOOD

ARIA COLE

One

Sadie

"Sadie fucking McGuire!" My best friend whipped around, eyes leveled on me. "You didn't tell me your boss was all kinds of fuck-hot!"

"Well, considering he's an asshole, I guess I *wouldn't* say that." I climbed out of the car and gave her a small wave. "Thanks for the ride to work. I swear I'll have my car fixed today, then no more rides."

"It's okay." She winked. "I like the eye candy around here."

I rolled my eyes. "I'm not sure when I'll be home. If you can't find me, you know I'll be here working on Lucy."

"Think you can score me the boss' number, too?" She leered.

I laughed with a shake of my head. "I'll do my best."

"Grow your hair out, put on some lip gloss—men like lip gloss. Makes them think about kissing you."

"I don't want him kissing me!" The truth was, I had thought about Jackson Fox kissing me, a lot. My hand involuntarily reached up to my short blond bob, fussing with it like I always did when I was uncomfortable. I'd never wanted long hair, short and sassy matched my style, but more importantly it was convenient. Suddenly I was thinking about Jackson's strong hands tugging on my hair as he bruised my lips with strong, soft kisses.

"Whatever. Prude." Ashley blew me a kiss as she backed out of the parking space. "Love you!"

"Yeah, yeah." I waved her off before turning to go into the office.

I'd only been working at Fox Motors for a few weeks. I'd had to cajole the owner and boss, Jackson Fox, to give me the job. It wasn't every day that a twenty-four-year-old woman walked into an auto body garage looking for work. But I was good at working on cars. I'd been doing it for years alongside my daddy, and I knew damn well I could show these guys a thing or two.

My mom hadn't been very pleased when I'd told her what I wanted to do. She'd said she didn't want a grease monkey for a daughter, but I didn't give a shit. I loved cars, I loved the sense of accomplishment in fixing something and bringing it back to life.

And after Daddy had died suddenly from a massive heart attack, it was the only thing I could bring myself to do. It felt like he was still with me. Being around cars was what my father and I had, and I never wanted to lose that. If I didn't have my head under a car's hood, I'd be hiding out in my room, depressed and dwelling on the loss of the only man I'd ever loved, the only man who'd ever cared for and protected me.

"Mornin', Sadie." Lowell, one of the other mechanics, greeted me.

"Morning." I smiled. "Get that Charger purrin' yesterday?"

"Purrin' like a kitten. Manifold needed work. Took me

a while to figure it out, but man it was worth it to hear her sing."

"I bet." I grinned, glancing at the cobalt-blue beauty parked in the front lot.

"Sadie." My boss, Jackson Fox, nodded as he came into the office.

"Hi." I looked away, feeling the intense dark eyes eating me up. Jackson had that way about him...that thing that drew women in like flies, had them flipping their hair and dropping their panties with just one crooked twitch of his sinful lips.

No wonder Ashley wanted his number. If I were a different girl, I would, too. But I wasn't the kind of girl men like Jackson went for. I avoided makeup most days, wore torn jeans, and kept my head down. Being a female in the auto industry meant I had something to prove. No way would I be the girl that dates the boss. I could just picture the guys snickering and saying how I fucked my way into a job, never mind that I was dedicated and amazing at it .

Not my style.

Chrome and leather, the smell of oil, and the weight of a wrench in my hand were my style. I knew I needed to work twice as hard to show these guys that I was the real deal.

"Slow day today." Jackson's voice vibrated with a deep timber. "Frank, can you take the oil changes? Got a chassis rebuild I want Sadie to work on with me."

"A rebuild? Me? What?" I asked, shocked. I'd helped my dad on a few engine rebuilds over the years, but never a chassis.

"Time you flex those muscles. Said you had experience, right?" Jackson's eyes cut to mine, holding me suspended in his intense gaze. How the hell would I get anything done working alongside him?

"Yeah, I just haven't worked on the chassis before."

"It shouldn't take more than a few hours," Jackson murmured, tossing a pile of paperwork on his desk before turning to the crew. "Sadie and I will be in the back garage if you need me, guys."

I swallowed, wondering what in the hell I was in for today.

I hated when Jackson singled me out, and he seemed to do it a lot in front of these guys. I didn't know if I was being too sensitive, but it felt like he was testing me, like he couldn't believe a girl would out-wrench a group of guys.

I knew I had the skills to prove him wrong, I just had to contain the erratic beat of my heart when he was next to me. It was hard to focus when Jackson Fox walked into a room. The little hairs on the back of my neck stood up, goosebumps pricked across my skin when his eyes landed on me, and that voice. Sweet lord in heaven, that voice was nothing short of sinful in the way it made my stomach coil and burn.

But I did have something to prove here, if not to him then certainly to myself.

No way would I let a man like Jackson Fox throw me off my course. I had dreams of opening my own body shop some day—McGuire Auto Body, after my dad. Working at Fox Motors was a priceless learning experience—picking up on the business side of fixing cars was something I didn't know how to do—but I was determined, and that had to count for something.

"You ready to get dirty?" Jackson came around the corner of his desk, fixing his gaze on me.

I sucked in a quick breath. "Always."

"Good. My kind of woman." His lips twitched. "Now let's get under that car."

I followed him out the office door and to the back of the garage.. The way his long legs carried him across the lot was nothing short of intriguing. The faded jeans hugging his hips and the broad cut of his shoulders with those massive biceps stretching the thin white cotton of his T-shirt were a mouthwatering distraction.

I wasn't sure why in the hell Jackson was working hands-on with me—until now he'd spent most of his days in the office handling scheduling and paperwork. But now he was here. With me.

What in the hell was I thinking?

My brain would short-circuit the minute he leaned over and asked me for a screwdriver.

Nothing about this job was easy, but working alongside Jackson Fox would make it almost impossible. I could only hope I didn't make a complete ass out of myself and get fired by the end of the day.

We stepped into the garage, my nerves on high alert already, before he turned, piercing me with his intense fucking eyes that stole all the breath in my body.

"Sadie…" The way his tongue curled around the word had the effect of his mouth fucking my name. My stomach fell into a dark pit, my nerves crawling with arousal, my thighs aching to shift back and forth to relieve the pounding desire between them.

"Yes?" I finally breathed.

Jackson took a step closer, his eyes burning up the contours of my face before settling on my irises. One hand rose, his thumb and finger brushing across my temple. "I hope you don't mind I pulled you today. I wanted to have some one-on-one time with you."

My heart ratcheted another dozen notches, no thoughts in my mind, only the urge to throw myself into his arms and taste his lips. "Oh...*kay*."

My brain ceased to function. It died a painless death right there on the floor of that garage.

"It can't be easy, being the only woman in the garage." His eyes trained on my lips, one hand settled at my neck, his thumb dragging across the hollow of my throat.

Oh Jesus.

Oh Jesus, Sadie. Get it together.

"I don't let it get to me," I uttered, my eyes focused on his. His own eyes watched my lips form the quiet words.

"I know you don't," Jackson muttered, leaning a little closer, his nose dusting the shell of my ear. My stomach flipped, my knees weak with every one of his movements. "Thing is, *Sadie*, I can't get you off my mind."

My fingers clutched at his steely forearms. His other hand weaved down the dip of my back, fingertips sliding just under the waistband of my jeans, making contact with my skin.

Jackson husked in my ear, "I'm bringing you home with me tonight and every night after."

Two

Jackson

"I keep imagining the taste of you on my lips." My fingers slid a little farther down the waistband of her jeans, those sexy fucking jeans that hugged her enticing curves, leaving me with a throbbing hard-on all day as I watched her work.

"Jackson," she gasped, her eyelids fluttering closed. She was so fucking sexy, so innocent, so completely fucking made for me I couldn't believe I finally had her under my hands. It'd been torture watching her these last few weeks. I even had a moment where I thought it was a mistake to hire her. A girl in the shop was one thing. A sexier-than-hell one was a whole other deal.

"The way you're rockin' your hips makes me think you want my tongue on you," I growled when I slipped my hand farther inside and found her ass cheeks completely bare. "You're wearing a thong, Sadie?"

She shook her head wildly..

"And this is?" I groaned, palming the flesh of her ass cheeks in my hand. So fucking sexy. My cock was rock hard and begging to cum deep inside her.

"Nothing... I wear nothing."

I couldn't see straight, certainly couldn't think straight after that. My lips crashed against hers as I lifted her against me. We careened against a wall, my hand supporting both of us as her lips parted and our tongues tangled together.

"Watching you bent over a car every day for the last six weeks has been fucking hell," I snarled, nestling my cock at the hot, wet source of all my of fantasies.

"I wondered why you gave me a dirty look every time I walked into the room."

"That wasn't a dirty look, baby. That was pain. You make my cock so fucking hard I could pound nails." Her breathing sped up, her hips rocking wildly until I spun us around, laying her across the hood of the car we were supposed to be fixing. "I've been dreaming of this pretty pussy since the second you walked into my garage."

My fingers stroked across the seam of her jeans—hot, damp arousal burning my fingertips and sending my brain into a frenzy. I pressed, rubbing around, where I imagined her clit was, dreaming of the time I'd get my lips on it. Our lips crashed together, her hands in my hair, running circles across my scalp before she tugged on the strands.

"So fuck me then," she purred, eyes riveted on mine in challenge.

"Jesus, don't tempt me, gorgeous." I trailed my tongue up her neck, imbibing the scent of her, desperate to see her crash in waves of pleasure on my hand.

"Since when are you so polite?" she teased.

I narrowed my eyes, my cock aching like it never had before, until I pushed a hand down the waistband of her pants and made contact with the searing flesh of her pussy. She arched and moaned, her fingers clutching the flesh at my shoulders.

"Oh God…harder."

"You're a sweet little surprise, aren't you?" I husked, speeding my fingers until I felt her thighs tensing around my palm.

"Oh my God…" she whispered desperately, her fingernails digging into my biceps. I slid my tongue past her lips, catching her groans before her muscles quaked and she came in a torrent around me. I sucked in deep breaths, trying to control myself as I watched her teeth clamp down on her bottom lip, stifling little moans I was desperate to hear.

"That's it, Sadie, give it to me." I eased my fingers out, letting her come down from her release. "I want all your orgasms from here on out." I fucked her mouth with my tongue, showing her how much I wanted her, how desperate I was to feel her, how she made me lose control like no one else ever had. "Got that?"

Her eyes fluttered open, her mouth curving in a small grin. "I got that, *boss*."

My eyes flared, my nostrils sucking in the sweet scent of her cum before I pulled a hand from her pants and thrust it between my lips. "Sweet as fucking candy, Sadie."

A blush crept up her cheeks before she straightened her hair, sliding up to a sitting position with her knees tucked between us.

"Ready to get to work?"

Her eyes shot open, wider than hubcaps, before she slid off the hood of the car. "I'm ready."

"Good." I smacked her on the ass, a cocky grin burning up my lips. "I like you ready for me."

Three

Sadie

My heart slammed against my ribcage as memories of his hands caressing my skin danced through my head. Jackson's touch was fire, a raging inferno that consumed my body and my mind. When he touched me all sense of reason evaporated into thin air and all I wanted was more--more heat, more sensation, *more Jackson*.

I had so little experience with men, but melting under his possessive fingertips had come shockingly easy. I was a certifiable tomboy. Men weren't often on my mind beyond the passing glance, a nod or an eye roll, depending on the day, but the way Jackson looked at me…like he wanted to eat me, I craved it. I felt alive when his eyes darted across my body. I felt like a woman, something that was tough to come by somedays when I was covered in oil and dirt.

I leaned over the hood of the car and with a final twist of a bolt, dropped the wrench on the workbench and stretched. All the muscles in my back ached. My shoulders and neck cramped from leaning for the last few hours. I trailed out of the garage, headed for the main office. I was still hoping if it was slow I could get a spare hour to work on my car. I hated relying on friends for transportation.

"All set." I pushed through the office door, not at all surprised to find Jackson alone, sitting behind his desk. But I was shocked beyond belief to see his throbbing dick in one hand.

"Oh." Air puffed from my lungs as my eyes zeroed in on the gorgeous, creamy tip of his thick erection.

Jackson's eyes flicked to mine, held for a minute, before his grin turned up recklessly. "Wanna take a seat?"

I pulled my bottom lip into my mouth, thinking I would do more than that. I locked the door and crossed the distance between us, dropping to my knees as I reached him and taking his cock into my hand. "I wanna taste you."

A virile groan released from his chest before his muscles slackened and he leaned back in the chair, eyes flicking across my face as I hovered at the tip, a shiny drop of pre-cum waiting for me.

"Been thinkin' about sliding my dick past your lips since the first time you smiled at me."

A small moan escaped my throat, my body flushing with desire, and I slid my lips down his cock. The way his body trembled and his hips jerked with the first touch of my lips sent arousal flooding between my legs. Jackson was one very good reason to wear panties to work. I'd have soaked jeans all day if he kept doing things like that to me.

"You're so big," I moaned, appreciating the incredible girth, the way the head stretched nearly to his navel. He had to be nine inches, at least. Nine inches of hot, smooth steel. What would he feel like pushing into me?

Could my body even accommodate him?

"You feel so goddamn good, Sadie." Both of his hands pushed into my hair, his hips rocking in slow motion, matching the rhythm of my mouth on his cock. "So beautiful, so sweet and young. I don't deserve you."

His fingers gripped my hair, and he pulled me up from my knees, leaning over to plant an earth-shattering kiss on my lips. "I've done my best to ignore your sweet ass bent over in my shop, but you've proven yourself unignorable."

His lips released me, I dropped back to my knees and my mouth fell back to his cock to swirl the tip, lick at the thick vein that ran up his gorgeous length. I fisted a hand at his base, my other sliding between his thighs to cup his heavy balls, so full of hot cum, all for me.

"Sadie, Jesus, Sadie…" His hips bucked with the first touch of my fingertips on his sac. Salty drips of pre-cum coated my tongue, I swallowed greedily, glancing up at the long, lean line of his neck as he clenched his jaw, looking like he was barely hanging on to his control.

"I've been so wet since the first time I saw you. I slide my hand between my thighs at night, thinking about the way your rough hands would feel gliding across my skin."

"I'm going to cum if you keep talkin' like that." His thighs were tense, one hand locked in my hair possessively and settling the ache for him a little deeper.

I cupped his sac in my palm, moving up and down his cock in a starved rhythm before my eyes flicked up and held his, intense and hot, like a wildfire between us. "Cum, Jackson. I want to taste you."

'Fuck!" he roared as long, hot jets of semen rushed down my throat. I sucked, milking him until all I could taste was him. I swallowed his unfamiliar, heady, and intoxicating essence, sliding off his dick and crawling into his lap. I straddled his powerful thighs, his wet cock still hard and twitching against my pussy. I placed a soft kiss on his lips. "You taste incredible."

Ragged breaths pulled at his chest, heaving and steady between me, our heartbeats thumping madly. I ran a hand across his laser-etched jawline. "I like when you're ready for me."

His eyes brightened, his lips curving up in a shit-eating grin. "Well, sadie aren't you the sexiest thing I have ever seen.."

He pulled my head to him, capturing my lips and thrusting his tongue into my mouth without reservation.

There was no need for him to ask permission, I was his. There hadn't been a single other person I'd thought about but him these last few weeks.

Sure he was a surly, moody, irritating asshole. But he was also gorgeous, kind, generous, thoughtful, helpful, and he wanted me. This man wanted me. At least for right now.

I didn't know what tomorrow might bring, but right now was pretty damn good.

Jackson released my lips, sliding his hands through my hair, pressing a palm to my cheek. "So fucking beautiful." He shook his head as if stunned. "I love fucking your mouth, precious, but next time I need to bury myself inside you. I want to claim this sweet cunt with every drop of my cum. You want my cum, Sadie?"

His fingers pressed between us, fingering my pussy through my jeans. "Yes…yes, please."

I looked up at him from under my eyelashes, and my belly burned and somersaulted like I'd never felt before.

I didn't know what this feeling was. I couldn't bear to put a name to it, but riding the high of Jackson Fox sounded like a pretty darn good idea at the moment.

"Go out to dinner with me tonight." He demanded it more than asked.

"I can't. I have to fix my car."

"Already did it." He lifted me from his lap, tucked his dick back in his jeans, then stood. "It's as good as new. Changed the oil, too."

"What? When?" I asked, shock and gratitude raining through me.

"While you were finishing up in the garage. That little Camry has over a hundred thousand miles. Not safe on all these country roads. We should get you something different." He flicked through the keyrings hanging on the wall behind his desk. "Want a Camaro?"

The keys dangled from his fingers in front of me. "You're insane."

"Insane to want to take care of my sexy Sadie? Hardly." He tossed the keys at me. I caught them, then instantly tossed them back.

"No, thanks. I like my car."

"Don't be crazy. It's on its last leg."

"I like it." I shrugged.

He narrowed his eyes, as if he was trying to read a book in another language, trying to decipher something that didn't quite make sense.

"Hotrods more your style? I've got a Maserati on the back lot you'd look hot as fuck in."

I laughed out loud this time. "No. Thanks for the offer, Jackson, but the Camry is perfect for me. Small, good on gas—"

"Rusted out."

"Shut up." I smacked at his shoulder, and he caught my wrist, pulling me against the hard wall of his chest. The air emptied from my lungs in a soft breath. He was so warm, so comforting and possessive, all in the same touch. He was exactly what I needed. I briefly imagined what it would feel like to give myself to him. To let go of the anxiety and the pressure to prove myself, and just be. All nerves and sensations, tongues and lips, the centuries-old way a man took care of a woman.

I yearned for that with every fiber of my being, and Jackson stirred the craving to life.

"So dinner? We can go back to my place, shower…get ready…" His hands crawled up my skin, landing at my shoulders and kneading gently.

"Mm… That feels so good." My eyes fell closed.

"I don't stand a chance of keeping my hands off you tonight if you keep makin' noises like that." His roughened voice wrapped around me.

"It's a good thing I like your hands right where they are." On me. In me. Demanding and all-consuming.

"Maybe we'll just have to stay in tonight, then," he murmured against my ear, sending shockwaves of desire racing through me.

"I like that plan better." I pushed up on my toes, wrapping my arms around his neck and kissing him again.

His hands went to my thighs, pulling me up around his waist and holding me against him as we kissed.

"You're gonna be the death of me, sweetheart."

Please enjoy the first three chapters of **Under**

Construction *on me! xo Aria*

UNDER

CONSTRUCTION

ARIA COLE

One

Paige

A soft grunt sounded through the wall of the neighboring apartment.

I crushed the pillow over my head, trying desperately to block out the stifled sounds of sex echoing through the wall.

Another one of those faint groans.

"God, I need to move," I groaned and rolled over, throwing another blanket over my head. The constant thud of a headboard kissing the wall my only reply.

"Please God, kill me now," I prayed.

The sound of fucking subsided, muted groans fading until it was silent altogether.

Thank God.

I sighed, throwing the pillow off my head, my hair snarled in a mess around my shoulders. The clock read one o'clock in the morning.

It was the second time this week this had happened. When I'd walked through this apartment six months ago, the apartment next door was empty. I hadn't even thought to ask about how the sound carried between the walls.

How could I?

This was my first apartment, my first time on my own. I'd lived with sorority sisters at the Kappa Alpha house off campus. But this…this was something else.

Despite all the fun I'd had in my college years, I was actually a pretty focused and responsible girl. I'd moved to the suburbs in the hopes of getting some quiet time, time to focus on case files, and get a full night's rest every night. Six thirty a.m. came quickly.

If this kept up for much longer, I'd have to look at moving. Could I break my lease?

I heard the pad of footsteps in the other apartment, gone for a few minutes, then back in the bedroom again. The sound of the shower running started next, and I breathed a sigh of relief, knowing this was the normal routine.

So predictable.

I tucked myself into my blanket, curling up with my pillow, and wondered not for the first time what my new neighbor looked like. Short? Fat? Tall? Dark hair? Blond? I'd hoped to catch a glimpse of him, but in the short week he'd been here, I'd been working late and he'd been working even later. I didn't hear his bootsteps down our shared hallway until after eleven p.m. Some nights long after I was in my pajamas, glasses perched on my nose, with a book in my hands.

The shower turned off a moment later, and I instantly chastised myself for not forcing myself into a deep sleep before he was out again. A few times after his shower, instead of falling right asleep he listened to ESPN highlights. *Loudly.* He did everything *loudly.*

I prayed tonight wasn't one of those nights.

I had an important case tomorrow, a surgery on a poodle that was something new and cutting edge. I was anxious to use some of the new equipment at the clinic. I'd spent hours, until my eyes were blurry, reading all the latest literature written by the other clinicians that were practicing these new methods.

I had to be well rested and awake tomorrow.

As my eyes finally shuttered closed, I hazily made a mental note that if Mr. Sex Machine next door kept me up another night, maybe I'd give him a taste of his own medicine.

Sure, it would be only me and my old and trusty vibrator, but I could give him a run for his money. If nothing else, at least I'd get an orgasm out of my revenge, and then I'd fall into a peaceful, sated sleep. Just like my dirty neighbor did.

Two

Stone

"Shit." I grunted, twisting the mailbox key in the damn impossibly small lock. I knocked one knuckle on the little metal door, hoping for a miracle to shake the key into the right position to open it. I'd been having a helluva time with it all week. I'd have to put a call in to the super about getting it fixed. I didn't have time for this shit. I worked long enough hours as it was.

"Son of a bi—"

"Just wiggle it," an amused voice chimed over my shoulder. "Here, let me."

Long, dark chocolate waves fell over one shoulder. High cheekbones and a beautiful heart-shaped face peered up at me. And then my eyes landed on her lips. Soft, plump lips that looked a little bit swollen, but not in that Hollywood overdone way. Nothing about her was overdone, she was all-natural and fucking gorgeous. I sucked in a quick breath, feeling a heat split deep in my stomach and radiate down through my balls.

Her little hand took the key from mine, jiggling it quickly, then like magic, the door popped open and revealed my mail—a sales flyer and a credit card offer.

"All that for junk mail." My lips curved up as her eyes landed on mine for the first time.

The deepest shade of green I'd ever seen peered up at me.

Fuck, who was this girl?

"I'm Stone. And you are?" I leaned a little closer, craving another whiff of her scent.

"Oh…" She paused, her eyes narrowing quickly. "You're the new neighbor!"

The irritation in her words was more amusing than anything. She was a livewire.

"You could call me that. I prefer Stone, though." I crossed my arms, leaning against the wall as my lips turned up at one corner.

She arched one eyebrow, shoving her own key in the lock, jiggling like she'd refined it to an art form, shoving her own stack of mail into the crook of her arm then slamming the little tin door, grumbling more to herself than me. "What kind of name is Stone anyway?"

I laughed. She was adorable, sexy as hell, and had a fire under her ass. And I liked asses. "Family name," I answered.

Her eyes nailed mine, narrowing into a dirty look. "Well, *Stone,* I've been meaning to talk to you."

"Oh?" I smiled, even more interested.

"Yeah." She paused, eyes darting down to my dirty, scuffed work boots, taking in the dust caked into my jeans, definitely lingering an extra-long moment when her eyes trailed up my torso.

I was a good-looking guy, I knew that, no cockiness about it. The thing was, I didn't have to work out. I worked hard and long in a job I loved doing physical labor. Fuck treadmills and weights. I shoveled, lifted, hauled cords of wood. I loved every second of it, but it wasn't until now that I wondered if this little firecracker in her cute little parrot scrubs was judging me.

"So what's on your mind, little bird?" She pursed her lips, clearly irritated with me. "Looks like you had a bad day. Wanna wind down with a drink with me?"

"What?!" She seethed. "No. No I don't. And I didn't have a bad day, I had a bad night, actually. Your…our walls are…"

Christ, she looked beautiful when she squirmed. "Thin?"

"Yes!" Her eyes shot up to mine. "Exactly. And I have to be to work early in the morning, so maybe if we could just be a little more aware of that…"

"Sure thing." I took another step closer, coming within inches of the soft, sweet curve of her neck. "Just as soon as you stop having wet dreams in the middle of the night. You wake me up with your moans. It's sexy as hell. So fucking sexy I can't get back to sleep after, and I have to fuck my hand to get you off my mind. I have to say, it was a bit hard conjuring a visual but now that the real deal is standing in front of me…"

I moved closer, fingers itching to touch, kiss, bruise, and claim every inch of her.

Her mouth rounded in an O, her eyes larger than the tires on my truck.

"Close your mouth, little bird. I'm a dirty man with an even dirtier mind." I tipped her chin up, pressing the seam of her dark red lips together. "It's going to be hard for me to get those lips out of my head tonight."

"You're…you've got to be…" She shook her head, finally giving up on putting words to exactly what I was.

"Not the last time you'll be at a loss of words around

me." I moved an inch closer to her ear, making sure my breath washed across her skin. "I'll take it as a compliment from you."

I winked, then passed her, pushing through the heavy doors and heading up the stairs to my apartment. I didn't even look back for her reaction.

Let her think on that one for a while.

Three

Paige
Him.
Him.
Stone. The fucking neighbor from hell with the overactive sex life, had kept me up all night.

I slammed the door of my apartment, not giving two shits if it rattled the walls in his damn place. I'd give him a run for his money. I'd show him how torturous it can be to live next to a sex maniac freak.

I threw my mail down on the kitchen table, then tore into my room, pulling the top of my uniform over my head and throwing it in the corner. I peeled down my pants, catching a glimpse of the stupid little parrots that decorated the fabric and remembering the way he'd called me *little bird*.

What a bastard.

I crawled into bed, making sure I bounced on it extra hard, enough so the headboard clattered against the wall a few times.

Fuck you, *Stone.*

I flipped over, yanking open the drawer on my side table and pulling out the tiny black bullet that I'd received at a bachelorette party. It was the only sex toy I owned, rarely used, but I was bound and determined to make good use of it tonight.

I flipped on the little motor, smiling when I heard it hum to life. I cranked the dial further, wishing the buzzing was loud enough to reach through the walls. Sliding the toy down my body, I hovered just above the crest of my pussy, dancing the little buzzing devil over my panties, and I hesitated.

This was immature, wasn't it?

Yes. But he was so damn arrogant. How could he move in and have no respect for the neighbors when I'd politely asked him to tone the fuck down?

A door slammed closed in the apartment behind my head.

Stone.

I fumed, wondering if replacing the batteries on my little pocket-sized boyfriend would make it buzz any louder.

No, that's your job.

Shit. I snuggled deeper into the fluffy blanket, spreading my thighs a little farther apart and touching the bullet to my pussy again.

I heard the bed squeak and shake just like it always did when he crawled into bed. But this was early. He definitely wasn't going to bed yet…was he?

I adjusted myself again, nerves eating up my stomach as I thought of his dark brown eyes, rimmed with thick eyelashes that cast shadows across his cheeks when his eyes squinted in laughter.

Yes, I'd noticed all that.

I'd also noticed that Stone was much sexier than any man ought to be. The broad biceps bulging through the thin white t-shirt he wore. The sharp cut of sexy muscle that stretched below his hips peeking out from his waistband when he'd shifted toward me. That glimpse of sun-kissed, golden flesh that promised so much more chiseled perfection hidden under a layer of cotton. The way the bold asshole had leaned in, whispering across my neck and leaving my panties damp for action they hadn't seen in far too long.

Vulgar groans emanated through the paper-thin walls, the creaking sound of a bed in movement shattering the bubble of desire that'd bloomed in my stomach.

"Dammit," I seethed, shaking my ass on the bed so the headboard would knock against the wall again.

The groans only grew louder.

I gritted my teeth, sitting up on my knees and placing the vibrator right against the goddamn wall, exactly where I imagined his big arrogant head would be. The vibrating head bumped and rattled against the wall, my grin growing wider as I imagined him fuming, his night surely ruined now.

I waited, trying to listen intently through the clattering of my sex toy, finally backing off to find the soft, erotic moans had only gotten quieter, but were still very present.

I rolled over on my bed, huffing as irritation pumped through my veins. I was determined to get my revenge on this arrogant asswipe.

I slipped the bullet under the elastic of my panties, holding it to my clit and instantly feeling arousal burn through my veins. My mouth popped open, and a soft sigh escaped.

I applied a little more pressure, exploring with the little textured head all the nerves between my legs. I allowed another moan to fall from my lips before I closed my eyes, dialing up the volume a few more notches and releasing another, even louder moan.

The sounds of sex from the other apartment died down instantly.

But it was too late, that magic little bullet of love had pushed me past the point of no return.

I clamped down on my lower lip, stifling loud moans as I swirled the head around my slit, sliding it down the seam of my damp lips, massaging my clit again, enjoying the slight bite of the nub as it kneaded my flesh.

"Oh my God, oh my God…" I groaned, hips arching as I clamped down on my lip again. I'd meant to put on a show, but I hadn't meant to get that loud.

But that little fucking bullet carried the secret to life, I was sure of it.

I hummed, one fist clutching at the sheets at my side, my other hand working the toy in tight circles at my clit. Jagged breaths cut with gasping moans filled the silence in my apartment as my toes curled, my back arching, my nipples hot and hard with built-up pressure, until… until…

Bam. Bam. Bam.

Someone was knocking on the door. I dropped the toy, cringing as it thudded loudly on the cherry wood floors.

"Fuck." I hopped out of bed, pulling a tank top and shorts on. "Coming!" I called, feigning casualness when I really wished I could ignore the door and finish what I'd started in the bedroom. Every nerve between my thighs flaming with warmth, begging and burning for the orgasm we'd worked so hard for.

"Who is it?" I breathed, unlocking the door and opening it without looking.

I should have looked.

If I had looked, I would have turned right around and gone back to my little magical friend.

But instead I opened the door and ran smack dab into the hard wall of his smooth, chiseled, naked chest. "Oh my God."

"Apparently," he growled, pushing through my doorway and slamming it on the hinges. "What's with the show, little bird?"

I crossed my arms, feet rooted as we squared off. "No show, just, ya know, having some fun."

"Fun?" His body entered my space, one hand landing on my hip, the other catching my wrist in his large palm. "Got a new friend?"

I turned fifty shades of red when he pulled the little bullet from my sweaty hand. I hadn't even realized I'd been clutching it so tightly. But that's what Stone did to me. He made me mad as hell, tense with irritation, wild with—

"I can make you cum harder than that little battery-operated bastard ever could." He tossed the vibrator on the couch.

"Look, I didn't mean to piss you off earlier, but those walls are really thin—"

"Don't I know it," he murmured against the crook of my neck. Jesus, what the fuck was that hot, wet, fucking amazing feeling crawling through my body? "I couldn't listen to those sexy little noises you were making a second longer."

I shuddered when his free hand trailed down my stomach, fingertips wisping against my body and causing rampant lightning bolts to catapult through me.

"Look at how perky those sweet little nipples are for

me," he whispered, blowing warm breath from his mouth over the needy little nubs, causing them to harden painfully, the outlines obvious through my soft cotton tank.

His hand slipped beneath the waistband of my shorts, and I instantly thought I should be stopping him.

Why the hell wasn't I stopping him?

I squirmed, running my hands over his carved shoulder blades. His thumb made contact with the outside of my underwear, directly over the hot little bud I'd been frantically working earlier, and a soft sigh tumbled out of my mouth.

"That's it, little bird. Let me hear those sexy little grunts now."

I clamped down on my lips, instantly self-conscious, but the desire pooling in my belly was much too strong to ignore for long.

"No, no. Don't get quiet on me now." His lips pressed against my ear. "You wanted me to hear the show, didn't you? Sing, little bird." His thumb applied more pressure to the bud of my clit, and then, with one swift grunt, he was shoving my cotton panties aside and making contact with my skin.

Warm, rough fingers meeting hot, aching, wet flesh.

"Oh God…"

"There she goes again," he whispered, pulling my head to his and swallowing the little grunts that were peeling past my lips. His hand worked swiftly between my legs, arousal pooling and dampening my thighs, his tongue thrusting past my lips. Another hand threaded in my tangle of curls, pulled at my hair as he pressed his lips to mine so fiercely I knew that they'd be swollen in the morning.

Evidence of where he'd been.

I secretly hoped they would.

"Bet this little pussy tastes even better than it smells." His filthy, unfiltered words wrapped around my ears, causing a spring to come uncoiled and shoot through every muscle of my body. I arched and rocked, riding my orgasm on his palm as I came harder and quicker than I ever had.

My knees softened to gelatin, my eyelids suddenly too heavy to hold their own weight. I clutched at Stone's shoulders, heaving as I breathed in the air at his neck. The sexy, spicy, earthy scent of him.

"Oh God."

"Mm…you're welcome." I heard the cocky tone of his voice. The way his lips curved up as he peered down at me only confirmed it.

Fucking Stone.

The neighbor from hell with the body of a Greek god and fingers so talented he could have told me he'd created the Sistine Chapel himself and I would have believed him.

How could I share a wall with him without thinking about his hand down my pants?

"Stone, I need to get to sleep, I think--"

"Got it, gorgeous." He caught my chin between his thumb and finger, planting a hungry kiss on my lips before backing away. "Have a good night."

The way his mouth curved up in that charming, rogue-ish, sort of maddening grin was the closest thing to swooning at a man's feet I'd ever been. What was this hold he had on me? Or more accurately, my body?

I crossed my arms, feeling a little uncomfortable, which was odd, considering how far he'd been already.

"Night, Stone."

"See ya, little bird." He swung the door closed behind him, before swinging it open again and ducking his head in. "Don't forget to lock this door behind me."

I grinned, feeling warmth pool in my belly. "Goodnight, Stone."

I pushed the door closed behind him, sliding the deadlock in place. I turned and let my body sink into the door, a unstoppable grin pulling at my cheeks.

Fucking *Stone.*

Acknowledgments

I have to thank my ever so loving and patient husband. You truly are my HEA, babe. < 3 Thank you to Aria's Assassins for keeping my fire burning. I am forever grateful for your love and cheerleading! I can't thank the ArdentProse team enough. You ladies make my life so much easier and I love you for it! To my ladies... the ladies that love to get lost in books about true and last lasting love... THANK YOU!!! Writing books you love is what keeps me going. You are my rock stars!

About the Author

Facebook

GoodReads

Twitter

Instagram

Newsletter

Also by Aria Cole

22650069R00063

Printed in Poland
by Amazon Fulfillment
Poland Sp. z o.o., Wrocław